Farewell

ADRIANA DARDAN

authorHOUSE®

AuthorHouse™
1663 Liberty Drive
Bloomington, IN 47403
www.authorhouse.com
Phone: 1 (800) 839-8640

Published by AuthorHouse 01/13/2017

ISBN: 978-1-5246-5905-9 (sc)
ISBN: 978-1-5246-5904-2 (e)

Print information available on the last page.

Contents

Dedication

To my family and to my friends who were always there for me with love, and grace, with trust, and understanding.

Adriana Dardan

Foreword

T HE STORY I am about to tell you can be developed anywhere in the world, without necessarily being anchored in a precise place with a bearing name. It can happen in any city with clean streets bordered with flowers and trees, with beautiful buildings habited by working people who water their lawns, where a park is the place for a relaxing stroll near a small lake, and where a green range of hills on the far side completes a surrounding of splendid scenery.

The characters in the story can also be found anywhere in the world, since they do not look different in habits and behavior from your friendly neighbors who greet you and smile every time you meet them.

The minute analysis of the characters in the story who confront difficult or gratifying circumstances, leads to a more enduring development of their personalities in rapport with each other, and to the conclusions reached by them, following many changes in their lives, on separate or common ways.

Nobody knows exactly how the human mind works. What science tells us is that our brain is a biological extremely complicated "neural network whose molecular mechanisms drive the formation of thousands of neural circuits, each wired for a specific behavior". In a metaphorical sense, it might be said that the human mind has a special design imagined like a delicate filigree that is strong enough to stand a most threatening storm, but can easily break at the touch of a painful spot deeply buried in the soul. Here comes the difference between people and the combination of traits that distinguishes the individual nature of a person. Our intrinsic feelings are by no one known, and therefore, they can be similar, different, or unique.

We can use again a metaphorical sense and imagine the mind as having the same design for every human being. Its activation on which way to take is everyone's choice. Average and normal people take one of the many paths opened for making their lives with dignity and fairness, by performing their duties, or making sacrifices for their faith and families. Other people choose the paths of an unstable behavior, by lying and stealing. Some others take the path of evil when only one spark of hate is enough to ignite the mechanism of violence and murder.

The choices made by the characters in the story, vary with the circumstances they encounter and which require day by day a careful decision according to the expected outcome.

The leading characters work a smooth path toward each other, with love, trust, and understanding, building a solid ground for a life meant to be filled with the best expectations one can hope for. Their feelings are stretched up from small emotions to great passions that are activated by memories, people, and events. When joy or suffering comes along, we must say that these particular feelings, both go together, side by side, and touch the same chord. All depends on the stimulus that is triggered by the mind and is activated first. The reaction to one or the other is linked to the circumstance that was encountered in the beginning. Here comes again a big difference between people when every one of them expresses a particular conduct to face one emotion or the other. In both cases if passion takes over and reaches a high level of action, it might become out of control, and many times, it is selected to be used as a mean of destruction. One step forward, the leading characters in the story, are confronted with a difficult situation when they have to take an extreme decision, either to go together on the consolidated path of their life, or go apart on different ways, far from each other. The choice they make will determine the progress of the story and will strongly influence the life of everyone involved and was close to them.

It is up to you, my Reader, to judge with fairness and not with disbelief the semblance of truth in the narrative and the conduct of the characters, their choices, and the decisions they made, along the development of this story.

Adriana Dardan

CHAPTER 1

I T WAS A warm sunny day with blue sky and a gentle breeze coming from the nearby park, bringing like a distant echo the twittering sounds of the buoyant birds that seemed to have a wonderful time. It was graduation day and the campus was crowded with families, friends, and people who probably had nothing better to do. The ceremony started few minutes before Ana arrived, and she barely could find a seat on the side, not too far from the stage. The Dean was performing a long speech embellished with many successes achieved by the graduates, and many suggestions for their future accomplishments. He also mentioned a few names of the graduates who excelled in their studies. Among them was Derek Milton, who became the most important being in Ana's life shortly after they started to know each other. It was one year ago when they first met at the library of the university where he consulted architectural materials, and she made researches in the Microbiology field. She let herself wandering in those memories when suddenly she heard his name. He took his diploma, shook hands with the Dean, and rushed off the stage, looking for her. There she was, the love of his life, waiting for him with stretched arms to embrace him, the man she treasured. They both were overwhelmed with joy.

"Show me your diploma", she whispered.

"It's just a sheet of paper that can open some doors for me", he said with a beautiful smile on his face. He was handsome, tall, athletic, with wavy, light brown hair, and hazel-greenish eyes. She looked at his diploma, congratulating him with a warm kiss. He suggested:

"Let's go to the park for a walk, and then after we go to a restaurant to celebrate. It's my treat."

Hand in hand, they went to the park all the way up to the lake, and sat down on a bench under an oak tree. Its name was the "Little Lake" and became a favorite site for people who wanted to relax by watching the parade of ducks going back and forth, displaying their gracious movements.

"You know what we celebrate today?" he asked.

"Of course. Your graduation which transfers your status from a little boy to a big boy."

"Wrong. Today we celebrate one year, two months, three weeks, and five hours since we met the first time."

"Four hours." She was more conservative, and she remembered only very well when they met the first time.

They kissed and looked at each other with tenderness and great affection. They understood each other's mind and soul; they shared opinions, choices, needs, plans, and everything that came into their lives. Their love had no dimensions, and no boundaries.

"You are so beautiful today", he said with a soft voice.

"I know."

She was not a so-called "beauty", but she was quite pretty to attract attention: average height, slender and graceful, blond hair, slightly curled and short cut, blue-grayish eyes, and very fine features; she was a most desirable combination of being very smart and charming. She was always well dressed, with simple clothes in elegant finery of good taste and very well tailored.

"What are your plans, from now on?" she asked.

"I received a proposal from a prestigious firm regarding a job as junior architect. It pays well, has good benefits, and the prospective to learn a lot and advance in my career are great. I accepted it. Before anything else, I have to look for a place to live, since I have to vacate my room on campus in less than a week."

More than anything, Ana would have liked him to move with her, but she had a small one-bedroom apartment at second floor, with no space to share. The building was located on a quiet street, with lots of trees and flowers on each side, in a very pleasant neighborhood, and had only four apartments. Ana's scholarship and part-time job were enough to support her modest life style. She could even save a very little bit of money from time to time. Her living room was crammed with books and stuff she needed for her studies and her bedroom was not big enough to accommodate two people. They talked about this alternative long ago, analyzing every single detail, and they both concluded that it was not workable.

"I'm so happy for you, that you already have a job! I think that you will love your work and you will be always successful in your career. I'm so happy, that my words are not enough to express how I feel."

He took her in his arms and kissed her eyes. They simply, adored each other.

"I shall build a palace for you, over there, on top of the hills. I solemnly promise you."

"I am touched and grateful, but rather I subscribe to a small, cozy, comfortable place. Now, can we go to eat something? Are you hungry?"

"Oh, I am. What would you like? French, Chinese, Thai, Italian?"

"Can you afford a hamburger with fries and a soda?"

"I most certainly can, my dearest Nitti."

Only he called her Nitti, and she had no idea how he came up with this name. They went to a small bistro, devoured their meal, and felt more refreshed. Both were very young and had a lot of energy to use without restraint. Derek was twenty-four years old, and Ana almost twenty-two. She still had one year to finish her Master degree in Immunology, after which she will have a full time job at the Research Institute where she worked now part time.

"Would you like me to come and help you packing your stuff?"

"No, dearest. Thank you kindly, but actually, there is not much to pack. Just a few clothes and books, some linen, my laptop, and my violin. If I find a nice place to live, I will buy whatever I will need. It was a long and exciting day for us both. I want you to go home and have a nice rest, and I'll call you later. Don't forget to love me, still."

"I will try."

They kissed and parted, each driving in a different direction.

Ana did not feel like studying that evening. She took a shower and went straight to bed. Actually, she only knew about Derek just the little he told her. His parents died in a plane crash when he was only six years of age, and his grandparents who lived in the city Heidelberg in south-west Germany raised him: Anton Weber was a surgeon and a native of Germany; Charlotte was French by origin, and she was a teacher. They both gave Derek a sturdy education and made sure that he will be prepared to face any hardship in his life. He came out an outstanding man with a great personality, who knew exactly how high to aim his ideals that could only be attained through hard work, discipline, and perseverance. After finishing high school, Derek decided to immigrate to the United States and pursue his studies in Architecture. He visited his grandparents occasionally. Ana never asked more details about his life, since she understood that if he only told her this much, it meant that he did not want any intrusion in his privacy. Not even from her.

In that evening, Derek was resting on his bed and lost himself in a reverie. She was all the best in his life and became everything he could dream of. Her parents were really charming and friendly people, and he liked them a lot. He knew that they liked him too. Her father, Matthew Landers, was the owner of a reputable Real Estate Agency, was very well educated, and liked to play piano. He also was very good looking. Her mother, Emily, was a nurse not only at the hospital, but also for the entire neighborhood, and she lent a shoulder to everybody who cried for any kind of help. She was a beautiful woman inside and outside. Besides, she was a terrific cook. Maybe because of her mother who talked so much about the incurable diseases of the patients she cared for, Ana chose to study the Immunology branch of Microbiology, hoping that her researches maybe in the future will help in finding eventual improvements, if not a cure. Derek not only adored her, but he admired her dedication, her mind, her great personality, and everything about her that inspired respect and a feeling of wonder. She was very knowledgeable about French literature, and they both liked Baudelaire and Verlaine. He called her:

"Good night, Nitti."

"Good night, Dery."

There was no need for more words. Ana decided to visit her parents the next day. She missed them a lot, and for the past two weeks, she could not find the right time to go and see them. With this thought in her mind, she fell asleep.

Her parents lived a few blocks far from Ana's place. They had a very comfortable house, surrounded by trees and flowers, with a very large back courtyard nicely landscaped and a swimming pool. Emily and Matt decided to keep Ana's room just the way it was before she moved out five years ago to pursue her studies at the university. Her desk was in the same place, and so were her bed and the nightstand. The walls were covered with small posters showing places from all over the world. Her books were carefully aligned on their shelves, and nothing was changed since she left. She was born there and grew up, being loved and cared for, by her parents, two people who would give their life for her. When she arrived at the doorsteps, her mother was already outside with both arms stretched to embrace her. Matt was in the kitchen, busy with something deliciously smelling, and preparing in the same time a plate with all sort of veggies that Ana always liked. She kissed her mother with great affection, and rushed to embrace her father. Every one wanted to talk first and tell the story about what was most important for each in the past weeks. They asked about Derek, and Ana told them about his successful graduation and about the new job he is about to start soon. When she talked about Derek, her eyes and face acquired a special warmth and brightness that openly displayed her great love for him. Both Emily and Matt liked him a lot, hoping for their daughter to have a happy life with him.

Ana left a few hours later, promising her parents to come next week with Derek. She went to the library for the rest of the day. Late in the evening, she called Derek and told him everything about her day. He was busy also, trying to find a place where to move.

After a few days, he came to see her and asked her to come for a drive. It was late afternoon and she still had many things to do, but she also needed a little time to relax. They drove about half an hour; he made a turn on a small, quiet street, with small, very nice houses on each side. They looked like the gingerbread little house from *Hänsel and Grethel, Grimm's* Fairy Tale. Derek stopped the car in front of one of them, and invited Ana to follow him to the front door. They stepped inside, and she was astounded. The two-bedroom house, with a living room with gas fireplace, and a small dining room next to the kitchen with a narrow door opening to a back veranda, completely surprised her. The rooms were furnished in antique style; one of the bedrooms was meant to be his study, in the middle of which was a Florentine desk, and the walls were covered with shelves filled with his books. Everywhere in the house, was Ana's picture. The dining table was set with fine china and silverware, and in the middle, a Japanese vase was displaying a bouquet of wild flowers, her favorites. Ana could only ask:

"How did you pay for all these?"

"From my Trust Fund."

Now she found again something she did not know about him. Maybe, in good time he will feel enough comfortable to tell her more about his life before they met. For now, she kept her attitude straight, by not asking questions and not searching for answers.

"Derek Milton, you never cease to amaze me. Everything is awesome."

"I'm so happy that you like it. I wanted to surprise you." His face was radiating his feelings. He took her in his arms and kissed her dearly.

"I made dinner, spaghetti and salad, and ice-cream, and soda, and coffee."

They were not hungry. Barely they touched the food, and had a small glass of white wine instead of soda. It seemed such a long time for both, since they met the first time!

Ana and Derek built their world from real and imaginary reveries, with sublime treasures by no one else known. The magnificent harmony of their understanding and feelings had no dimensions and could be measured only by the same powerful innermost values of their minds, their aspirations, and their affinity for each other. The sensory constituents of their entities developed together moving toward the same ideal where their souls and bodies became one.

He woke up first early in the morning, and let her sleep a little longer. In the kitchen, he prepared a healthy breakfast, since he knew that they were both hungry.

She came all dressed up, took his face into her hands, and kissed his eyes.

"Good morning, dearest."

"Good morning, my love."

Derek prepared the most important question in his life, and anticipated all the follow-up answers.

"Ana Landers, will you merry me?"

"No. You know very well that I have to finish school and work on my Master thesis. I also have to keep my part-time job at the Laboratory since I intend to work there, later as a full-time researcher. Being married now, will be a hardship for me, instead of the beginning of my happiness. Let's wait for a little while, just to do the right ting at the right time."

"I understand, and I respect your decision. I will wait, but without patience."

He drove her home, and he went to the gym for his workout session. No matter how many tasks required his attention every day, three times a week he performed his workout to keep himself in a healthy shape. Sometimes, Ana joined him, and he liked to act as her trainer. In spite of her body looking slim and frail, actually it was very strong, indeed.

In a couple of days, Derek will start his job and he promised to himself to be the best in his team. Until then, he wanted to meet Fred Williams, his friend from the first year in college, when they shared the same room on campus, and enjoyed many outside activities. They used to play lots of pranks and tricks to girls, jut to attract their attention, and many times, they got into trouble. They both had a few casual relationships, but nothing to last for a longer time. Still, Fred remained very closely attached to his high school sweetheart Ashley, to whom he was engaged for already two years, not being decided yet when to get married. They both graduated in Business Administration and made a very good living in Marketing. Ana met them and she liked them from the first sight. They became her friends too in a very short time.

Derek called his friend; they met at the same familiar Bistro, frequented by them both since they were young students looking for a place to chat and spending a good time with lighthearted girls. They gave each other a big hug and had a big smile. Fred asked:

"How have you been lately, old pal?"

"Good, very busy." Derek told his friend about the job he was going to start soon, hoping to achieve a prosperous career. It was his turn to ask:

"How about you and Ashley?"

"Very well, trying to make money in Marketing and both working for the same company where the commissions are really great. How is Ana?"

"Studying for her Master degree. She is fine; working hard to succeed in what she likes the most, namely, science in the research field." This much was enough for Fred to know. Derek never disclosed what he considered being personal and belonging only to him. He never allowed anyone to touch even by far, what he believed was too sensitive and intimate, as to be shared with people who appreciate only superficial conversation. Fred was quite different; he liked to talk about everything was going in his life, no matter how casual or personal the subject of discussion was.

They had a long chat about the good times they both had in college, and how they became good friends over the years. When ready to live, Fred said:

"In about two weeks, I'm not sure of the date, Ashley wants to throw a party, to celebrate our two years of engagement. There will be many of our colleagues from work and some from college. You and Ana are on the top list of her guests and you are invited to join our cheerful event. I'll call you to let you know the exact date. Promise to come?"

"Thank you, but I have to talk to Ana first, and see what her schedule is."

They gave each other a big hug again, hoping to meet another time for a long chat about many other different subjects that were familiar to them both, and were just enough to make a casual conversation. It was already late evening when Derek went to see Ana.

"You look exhausted", he said. "Did you eat anything today?"

"I guess, I did."

"When will you start taking care of yourself?"

"Tomorrow. How was your meeting with Fred? How are they both doing?"

"Not now. I'll tell you some other time. Now you need rest and you are going to sleep." He put her to bed, and kissed her dearly.

"I loved you all day long".

"That's comfortable to know."

"Good night, Nitti."

"Good night, Dery."

He turned off the lights, locked the door with his own key, and went straight home. On the way, he was thinking that she worked too hard and looked tired. He will find something to make her life easier; even if he knew very well that for the time being it was nothing he could do.

Derek started his first day on the job as the youngest member of a team of six architects and four designers. The boss introduced him to his new colleagues and showed him to his place, in a corner of the big room where a desk with a computer and all the requisites were provided for him. It took Derek only one hour to get accustomed with the project and to start working right away. He liked the place and his colleagues, and the project he was assigned to, looked interesting.

In the same time, Ana was working on her project in the laboratory, sharing the results found under the ultra microscope with the two researchers next to her, who had a lot of experience and from whom she could learn a lot. She was the youngest of the team and very appreciated for her dedication and knowledge. Her flexible schedule allowed her to work aside the studies for her Master thesis, but never missing to achieve in due time the part of the project assigned to her. One year ago, the Director of the Institute, Doctor Jason Blake, well renowned scientist and researcher with many big contributions to Immunology, who also was her Professor at the university, recommended her to the job. Ana tried to avoid him, because every time they met, he kept persuading her to follow her vocation for research by enrolling in a doctoral degree program. Just the other day, he asked her again:

"Did you make up your mind?"

"I'm still thinking. As I told you so many times, the program takes a long time to be accomplished, and I intend rather to start a family of my own. Besides, I am happy with a Master degree and I like my job just the way it is."

"You don't know very well your mind, girl. You are born to be a scientist; you have a special capacity to dissect minute details, a great gift that too many illustrious scientists and researchers are lacking. You can bring great contributions to improvements regarding the human life and to research regarding much too many diseases that have no cure. Don't waste it."

Ana struggled hard in her thoughts about that sensitive subject without being capable to take the right decision. One thing she knew for sure, was that she would not be able to accomplish both her ideals: family and doctoral degree. Neither Derek, nor her parents knew anything about she was going through. It was up to her only to make a choice, to take a decision, and to live for the rest of her life with the dilemma of her mind. Maybe, sometime later, the conclusion she was looking for, it will show up by itself.

Concentrated on her work, Ana did not hear the secretary of Doctor Blake approaching from behind.

Her name was Ellen Edelborg, but every one called her *Miss Marple*, like Agatha Christie's sleuth, because she knew everything about everybody, including family, relationships, and hobbies. She was with the boss since the first days of the Institute, about twenty years ago.

"Your love called", she whispered to Ana, "and he expect you to come over to his house. He will make dinner."

"How do you know?"

"Because I asked."

Behind her mask, Ana had a short laugh.

"Thank you Miss Marple."

"Don't mention. You know I like Derek."

She left quietly, just the way she came. There were not allowed phone calls in or out, and nobody could enter the establishment without appointment approved and set by Miss Marple. She took the phone calls for every employee and delivered the messages, adding her own commentaries.

Late, after work, Ana drove to Derek's house. He was waiting for her with big impatience to tell her everything about his first day on the job. After embracing and kissing her with passion, he told her that he liked a lot the place, the project, and his colleagues who were friendly and communicative.

"Poor guys", Ana said, "they have no idea what is coming in their future. Your potential and your ambition to succeed will leave them all far behind in a very short time, and then, they will not look so friendly and communicative."

Derek was very pleased with her remark and promised not to disappoint her.

"Make sure though, to play straight and fair. I'm convinced that you'll be honest as you usually are", she added.

"You know I'll behave like a gentleman, and I'll never do what you won't. What would you like for dinner? I did not have time to cook, and I must order something to please your taste. Make your choice."

"A juicy hamburger with fries and a sip of white wine."

He placed the order on the phone, and in the meantime, they sat at the fireplace with a small glass of white wine.

"Play something for me, Dery."

He took his violin and played for her Rimsky Korsakov's the violin solo from *Scheherazade*. She kept looking at him and could not detach her eyes from his face. He was transfigured and completely like living into another world. His eyes showed a light of serenity alternating with a fire of big struggles. He played the harmony of love and the outburst of passion. She could not tell what turmoil was concealed by his mind in those moments. He could have been a virtuoso violin player and had he become one, he could have covered with tears his audience. She played piano too, but not the same as he played his violin. His passion was tremendous, and if by any mischance it would come out of control, it will take only a split second to be converted into a very dangerous expression of his deepest feelings.

They both kept a deep silence after he finished. There were no words to describe their feelings, and there was no need for any words. Many times, she asked him to play the violin for her. He had an impressive repertoire and knew already what she liked the most.

The next day, he went to work, and she went to the library. Only late evening they talked a lot on the phone, telling each other about their day.

"Good night, Dery."

"Good night, Nitti."

One evening he took his recorder and asked her to say something, so that he could have her voice with him, all the time and everywhere he goes. She said:

"I want to listen to the warmth of your soul and feel the wonders of the stars in your love for me."

Derek was so moved that he forgot to turn off the recorder. She had to do it.

A few days later, Fred called Derek reminding him about Ashley's party. Derek forgot all about it and he never mentioned to Ana the big event that was supposed to be celebrated by their friends. He will give Fred an answer tonight, he said, after he will talk with Ana. He told her and was surprised by the easy way she accepted the invitation.

"Are you sure that you want us to go?"

"Of course, I'm sure. There will be many of our friends and colleagues there, and besides, I did not see Ashley in a long time. Occasionally, I miss her fast-talking about little things that make little sense and have little significance. She is very refreshing when she is not quarreling with Fred. Don't you want to go?"

"Yes, I want to, and maybe who knows, we'll have a good time."

After a couple of days, Derek went to pick up Ana for the party. On the way, they bought a box of sweets and a bottle of expensive wine, and arrived at the address later than the other guests. Fred's house was on the outskirts of the city, and looked impressive, like a mansion with beautiful landscape, swimming pool, and tennis court. The front door was open and they entered inside. The large room was packed with people, all cheerful, talking, laughing, dancing, and having a good time. The music was terribly loud and most appropriate for that event, according to the hosts' particular style, namely, it was rock-and-roll played through high speakers, which made almost impossible to hear the words of someone talking even nearby. A long table next to the facing wall was covered with appetizers, snacks, and beverages. They looked for familiar faces, but could not see any. Maybe their common friends and colleagues had no time for attending the party. Both Fred and Ashley rushed to greet Derek and Ana. The four of them barely could find a place to sit; they have a lot to talk about what each of them did lately, but only a few words they could exchange because the noise was deafening. Ashley suggested using the study room where they could have more privacy.

"We invited almost everybody we knew, but I think the crowd is too large and some of our guests feel uncomfortable", Fred said.

"Many are our friends, but most of them are business partners and we need them every day for the transactions that make the money flowing", said Ashley, and she asked, "how are you two guys doing?"

"Fine, thank you", answered Derek.

"Nothing unusual, just daily routine", said Ana.

A long pause followed and then Ashley continued:

"This is the second anniversary of our engagement, and maybe we'll decide to get married soon; not exactly because we are curious about the big event, but it will help our relation from many angles and points of view. How about you two?"

"We will let you know", answered Derek.

The conversation started lingering a sense of tedium. Ashley told them about her most exciting activities, with friends and relatives, about her desire to take a trip overseas, about buying a cabin on the other side of the hills close to the Big Lake, where she could watch the small boats and the ferryboat. She chattered about everything crossing her hyperactive mind in those moments. Now and then, she mentioned Fred's name too.

"Let's go mingle with the crowd", she said, and then added, "maybe, you'll come to dinner sometime, and we'll have a nice chat over a lobster feast and champagne."

There was no reply; just a friendly smile. They went back to the main room where people showed their expansive needs to dance and make lots of noise. Derek whispered:

"Let's go home, Nitti. Nobody will notice".

Ana nodded her head in approval, and they left. It was a quiet night with trillions of stars shining over a world that kept changing all the time for better or for worse.

They arrived at Ana's apartment, went upstairs when Derek said:

"I'm famished."

"I will make something to eat. I'm hungry too."

She made some sandwiches and a small salad. He was watching her and said:

"I'm glad we are not like them. Both Fred and Ashley changed a lot lately. They are not anymore the people we knew years before."

"You think they love each other?" she asked.

"Hmm... hard to tell. I believe the only bond between them is money. That is what keeps them together and makes them alike. They are surrounded by people with same interests that have no feelings for what is really valuable in life."

"You know something?" Ana asked, and she continued "I live most of the time among people wearing masks and white coats who move like ghosts around me in the lab; or among lifeless people staring at words and pages in books, without moving at all in the library. I feel like going somewhere for a change, and be among alive people who talk, laugh, stroll, and look happy. I was thinking if you would like us to go Sunday to the Big Lake and enjoy a bit of sunshine and fresh air on the peer, and have a tour with the ferryboat. That is if you are not busy and your work schedule allows you to have a little free time."

"It's a date. I will be happy for us to have such a short but rewarding relaxation and enjoyment."

It was already late night when they went to bed. The next morning Ana woke up first and prepared breakfast and strong coffee.

"I'll call you in my lunch time to know how you are doing."

"Miss Marple will be delighted. She said that your voice sounds like a violoncello. Did you sing in her ears?"

"No, but I will. I will sing for her 'L'air des clochettes' from *Lakmé*."

Ana exploded into a contagious laugh.

"Try 'Rigoletto'. It will suit your voice splendidly. She'll be moved to tears. Maybe tomorrow, because today I will be in the library, and we'll talk late evening when I will be home."

"You're not seeing your microbes today? Are you neglecting them?"

"Don't start."

He put his arms around her shoulders and looked deep in her eyes. His voice was soft and calm, but categorical:

"Ana Landers, you are the most intelligent person I know. I love you like no one in this world, and I greatly admire and respect your dedication and your work. Sometimes your obsession for the subjects of your research becomes over sized, and I sense in those moments a heavy storm in your mind that can easily burst out and threaten your health. This is the reason I tease you now and then, just to trigger a short circuit between your deeply immersed concentration on your work and the real world outside your electronic microscope."

She looked at him like always in those moments when he was the only thought in her mind, and whispered:

"Derek Milton, you have no idea how much I treasure your concern about me, and how much I love you. Now, you may kiss me."

In those moments, their feelings and their souls merged into one single entity.

He went to his office and she went to the library. Derek had a tied schedule and he had to finish in short time his part of work that was crucial for the whole project. He took some of the plans at home to complete the details of his assignment. That night he slept only a couple of hours, and the following night he did not sleep at all. Everything was ready to be submitted Monday, first thing in the morning. The next day was Sunday and he rushed to Ana's place to pick her up for the big day they planned to spend among "alive people who talk, laugh, stroll, and look happy". She was waiting for him, dressed like for camping, and with a big smile on her face.

"I missed you. Are you ready for the big event?"

"I am indeed, and I intend to enjoy every minute. I missed you a lot, as always."

The road was clear and smooth, with not a big traffic. It took them about one hour to get there. They went to the peer, and indeed, people were strolling, looked relaxed and having a good time. They were alive, as Ana expected, and they were behaving like pertaining to the real world. There were lots of small boats and canoes floating up and down over the lake. The entire surrounding was filled with an atmosphere of elation, where people forgot for a little while about their worries, problems, work, and duties.

Ana and Derek became part of that scenario which called for relaxation, and a delightful great time. They went to the site where the ferryboat was waiting for passengers to be boarding in approximately ten minutes. Everybody was looking for a seat on the upper floor, to have a better view of the entire scenery rich with colorful sailboats, and farther away with the display of the forest along the shore. The entire trip took about one hour along the lake and everybody on board had a tremendous time never to forget.

They both were hungry, looking for a cozy place to eat, close to the shore. They found a small family diner with a charming deck outside displaying a few tables covered with white tablecloths, not far from the peer. The food and service were excellent and much appreciated. It was almost late evening when they decided to return home. Both were surprised by the tan of their skin just being exposed to the sun for only a few hours. Certainly, they looked healthier and in a very good shape, if not mentioning the great disposition of their feelings. It took them another hour on the way back to Ana's place.

Derek accompanied her to the door, made sure that everything was all right, and was prepared to leave, when she asked:

"You are not staying?"

"No dear. I have to get up very early and go the office, because is the due date for the project I was working lately."

Her mind trained to dissect minute details, sensed a particle of dust floating in the air. She took his face into her hands, and looked in his eyes:

"Talk."

"About what?"

"About what has to be talked."

He never could resist her when she was like that: a mixture of being soft, caring, loving, and terribly authoritative. He told her in details about everything regarding his work, and the nights without sleep he spent to finish his part of the job. She only looked at him, saying nothing for the time being. He will find out in the morning when he will be awake enough and able to understand her site. She helped him undress, put on his pajamas, and covered him with the comforter. Before she kissed his forehead, he was already asleep.

Ana made her bed on the couch, thinking that he behaved like he said, only to make her day as she wanted, to spend time among "alive people who talk, laugh, stroll, and look happy". He woke up in the morning, all invigorated and in very good mood.

"Why did you sleep on the couch?"

"Guess. Why didn't you tell me about your busy schedule? We could have postponed our relaxation trip until next Sunday. Do not under estimate my capability of understanding the priorities in your life."

"You are my priority, and I'll do it again. It was nothing to postpone. I have to run now, and I'll call you. Bye, my dearest."

He did not want to prolong that conversation because he knew that she was right.

After a few days, Derek applied for his Architect license. He met all the requirements and passed the exam without any difficulty. Shortly after, he was promoted to senior Architect and was awarded with a substantial increase of his salary. He could not wait to tell Ana.

Late evening he showed up at her door with a bouquet of wild flowers.

"You can't bribe me with this", she said, and "What did you do this time? Do you intend to move to the outer space, and take me with you, maybe?"

He took her into his arms, kissed her, and told her about his great performance.

"I even got a place at the windows, with a big desk, and a high chair. Are you happy for me, that is, for us both?"

"I am more than happy. I know how hard you work, how good you are at your job, and how much you deserve to be appreciated and rewarded."

It was her turn to kiss him and caress his beautiful face. They always shared everything they had and achieved, without hiding anything from each other that made them happy.

"I am hungry", he said, "what do you have?"

"Sandwiches or fried chicken, or both."

"Not good enough. I will order steaks with backed potatoes, and chocolate cake."

They talked a lot about jobs and perspectives, avoiding touching the sensitive subject of making plans for them being together, other than they were.

The following Sunday they went to visit Ana's parents. Both Emily and Matthew were enthusiastic to see them. After a rich dinner, Derek asked Matthew for a private discussion and they both went to the study, living Ana and Emily to chat about what they did since the last time they saw each other.

On the way back home, Ana asked Derek about his conversation with her father. He said that he needed some advice regarding a lot on the outskirts of the city, which one of the clients of the firm chose for building his house. Ana did not believe one word of what he said, but kept quiet, just to avoid a squabble over something she considered of being not important for her. She was thinking that eventually, she certainly would find out what this was all about, if that subject will show up again on the stage.

"We are going to my place and I will show you the model I'm working on."

"Take me home, Dery. I have to be very early in the morning at the lab, to finish a task that was given to me quite long ago. We'll talk tomorrow."

Ana could not fall asleep. Her mind was turning on all sides the results of her research that seemed to have a slacked interpretation of a detail, and somehow she missed it. She checked several times the last *Petri* dish with the sample, which was supposed to conclude the research, but in the last reading, she assumed a prior condition that was wrong.

She went to the lab very early in the morning, assembled all the notes written before, and read them repeatedly. She worked several hours in a row, changing procedure and chemical solutions, and finally she found the missing link: the amount of a chemical was very slightly not in the right proportion in relation with the whole. It had to be adjusted to work properly for the right result. The conclusion became evident and flawless. Ana could write with big confidence a very well documented paper, and presented it to the boss. He was extremely pleased, since that part of her research was essential to the next step for a new approach to improve a certain vaccine.

In that day, Ana skipped her study in the library. It was a lot of material to work for her Master thesis but she had enough time to finish it. Besides, her advisor assigned by the faculty supervised her work closely, making sure that she meets the due date for each stage. The subject of her thesis in the field of *"Synthesis of exosomal structures"* was extremely interesting and challenging. She was very pleased with the progress of her work.

It was late evening when she went home, took a shower, ate a few crackers, the only meal she had since morning, and went to bed. Derek called late, but she was too tired for a description of the roiled activity of her day. He understood.

"Good night, Nitti."

"Good night, Dery."

Ana's next day was wholly committed to the research studies in the library for a special part that had to be included in her Master thesis. In the meantime, Derek moved his model to the workshop of his office, since it was more comfortable for him to work there rather than at home.

It was already the end of October; it was snowing, with big flakes that displayed their beauty just for seconds before reaching the ground. Ana was looking at the snow outside, while Derek was sitting on the couch, listening to one of Chopin's *Ballade*.

"Emi called and said not to make any plans for Christmas, because they both want us to come over and celebrate Christmas Eve with them."

"Mom? Why didn't she call me?"

"Because, my dear, you never can be reached. You are doing research either in your lab, or in the library. In the evening you go directly to bed because you are exhausted."

She kept staring at the snow outside. "I lose him", she thought. She saw herself ending up as a spinster looking for a mate in a *Petri* dish. Suddenly, she solved the long time dilemma about her enrolment in the doctoral degree program, and felt a great relief. She turned around and looked at him:

"Bear with me until June, when I have to defend my thesis. After that, we both take vacation and make a trip somewhere we both like."

It was an unexpected reaction for Derek. He was prepared for un unpleasant confrontation followed by regrets on both sides. Taking her in his arms, he only asked:

"Where to?"

Derek was familiar with Europe, and when she was a teenager Ana and her parents visited London, Paris, and Rome. It would be their first vacation and she wanted them to go somewhere to a pleasant region and to avoid crowded places and big cities with noise and polluted air.

"Belize. There is a sub-tropical climate, with mild temperature throughout the year, long beaches, beautiful landscapes, fresh air, original culture, sites of Mayan civilization, and lots of peaceful surroundings."

"You don't know how much this means to me. I can wait with patience until then. Promise."

Christmas was already there, and they went to the house of Ana's parents for the big celebration of the holiday. Two couples, friends of the Landers' were already there. A huge Christmas tree beautifully decorated, was displaying a rich atmosphere of joyfulness and colorful harmony. Under the tree, many presents for each waited only to be opened. The diner was abundant in delicious dishes, wine, and deserts, to please everyone's taste. Both Matthew and Emily with the help of their housekeeper were working the entire day to make the best of a wonderful celebration for their precious guests.

Ana and Derek left very late night, and spent the rest of it at Ana's place. The Christmas season was as usually, a time when people loosen their focus upon working and rather like to prolong their coffee and lunch breaks with nice chats over small snacks that are displayed everywhere on tables and desks. Even the management joined in the pleasant atmosphere of the holidays. All the institutions were closed three days for Christmas and a couple of days for the New Year, which gave Ana the opportunity to advance a lot in writing her paper for her thesis. They both spent the New Year's Eve at Derek's house, talking a lot about the great time they will have in the vacation waiting for them, as they planned.

Time went by, day by day, and week by week. Spring was already there, with sweet fragrances of blossoming flowers floating in the air. One evening Derek asked Ana:

"When can you make a little time and go with me for a ride?"

"Tomorrow I can spend a few leisure hours, since I gave today my paper to my advisor to read it and make his comments. Where do you want us to go?"

"Just for a pleasant drive, to enjoy the beauty of nature and the splendors of the spring. I will pick you up around noon."

"Sounds very good to me. I must add though, that the real beauty of nature resides underneath of what we see with naked eyes, and which starts with the subatomic particles of the microstructure of the world."

"Spare me the details. I am very happy with the visible reality, just the way it is displayed before my eyes, and actually, I do not want to see what is underneath a world that might even scare me, and I might not even like it. Your notion about beauty is totally distorted."

They both had a tremendous laughter. Next day around noon, he was at the door of the Institute and picked her up. On the way, Ana tried without success to make him talk about the destination of that ride. He changed the subject all the time and made jokes about everything that was not touching her obsession with the underworld creatures. After more than one hour of driving, he took a narrow road to the hills and stopped the car in front of a large area covered with grass and flanked by trees on both sides. The land was a quite flat ground, like a small plateau between two crests of the hills. Two impressive houses, one of each side, quite far from the borders displayed a rich design of that property. Both were at a lower ground level. A splendid view of the Big Lake down the hills was completing a scenery that could be described only in movies.

"This is a really outstanding view and place", Ana said. "If you wanted us to come for a picnic, you should have told me and I could have prepared some sandwiches and drinks."

"I bought this place."

"Whaaat? Wheen? Hoow?" she kept asking, barely breathing, looking around in amazement.

He just could not enjoy more the expression of astonishment on her face.

"Matt found it after many attempts to reach the best land and location. Remember months ago when I asked him for a private conversation in his study? I told him what I wanted and he promised to look for something outstanding. He also was sworn to secrecy."

She remembered very well that day when he looked like hiding something from her, but she did not insist in finding what. He continued:

"I will build your palace here, my dearest love. I promised you so. Remember?"

She remembered, all right. It was the happy day of his graduation when he made that solemn promise. Now, he was staring at her continuous amazement, and intended to intensify it even more. A very small velvety box was in his hand. He opened it and took out a superb, gold pendant, with a fine, exquisite design, and with two small diamonds touching each other. On the back was only one word inscribed: *Forever.* He put it around her neck and said:

"I know that you are not supposed to wear rings. I bestow upon you this pendant as my crest of love that is forever."

Ana kissed it with a feeling of deep warmth. She had tears in her eyes. She just became incapable of saying one word. He never saw her crying and she rarely cried and only when she was alone. All that excitement was too much for her to react in either way. She only ran into his arms and cried. He understood her big emotions and at his turn, he could not utter any word, since he was deeply touched by her feelings.

"This place needs a name", he said. "Would you like to name it after one of your microbes?", and he laughed.

"No. You will not remember it. You choose the name."

"How about 'Eden'?"

"Like the terrestrial paradise with many delights, where the first man and the first woman were placed by the Creator? I like very much this name."

"Eden it is!" he shouted so loud that maybe people in those neighboring houses heard him. A woman came outside, waving her hand to them. Derek waved back, jumping up and down like a small child who received a toy.

Late evening they returned to their daily realities and went to Derek's home. They decided for the coming Sunday to have a picnic up there, walk on the grass, and have a closer look at the land.

The next day Derek went to the building site with the construction engineer to meet with the supervisor and the crew to analyze the plans for the new house. He finished the model he was working on for so long, and took it with him. The measurements for the foundation were already taken and the work had to be started. He spent there almost the entire day making sure that no detail will be overlooked.

Ana did not have to go to the library in that day. Her advisor read her paper, made a couple of comments, and was very pleased with the progress she made. She spent her entire day in the lab, starting her new assignment in the field of *Viral Vectors and Gene Therapy.* It was a tedious job requiring her entire concentration and a lot of knowledge, since Immunology in that regard was a threshold for finding new ways of research and a lot of study in that particular field.

Whenever she had the occasion to take a break, Ana touched with warmth and treasured memory the gold pendant attached to the chain around her neck. In that evening, Ana called her mother and told her everything about the place in the hills. Emily already knew from Matt, whose sworn secrecy always stopped at his wife door. She wanted very much to see that wonderful place, but maybe later, when she will be able to take a short break from her duties at the hospital.

Next Sunday, Ana and Derek drove up to the hills for the picnic as they planned. Ana brought a blanket and a basket with food, while Derek brought his music player. On the way they talked a lot about the house he intends to build.

"I'll start the design very soon and have to work the plans at home, whenever my time will allow. My good friend and colleague Willie Reiss, is the best constructor engineer I know, and he will be my choice for this project. He is a native from Germany, like me, and made his studies here, finishing them about ten years ago. You should meet him and his wife Linda who is a teacher. I am sure you will like them both. They have two teenage girls, very well educated but a little frivolous, in my opinion."

"I can't wait to meet them. If they are your friends, they will be mine too."

He stopped the car, and they walked to the same place they went before. The weather was very pleasant, with blue sky and many flower fragrances floating in the air. Derek put a soft music, and asked:

"Shall we dance?"

"Is this the right place for dancing? Do you have chiming bells in your head?"

"Yes. Come, dance with me."

They danced like in a ballroom, with elegance and graceful movements. Both were marvelous dancers.

"I would prefer a floor, but grass is alright and actually, not bad at all", Ana said.

A couple from the house on the right site saw them and waved their hands. Derek shouted so loud with his baritone voice, that probably people down in the city could hear him:

"Hi, I am Derek and this is Ana, my fiancée! We bought this place!"

"Do not push it", Ana whispered, "Since when am I your fiancée?"

The man said with a loud voice:

"Hi, Ana and Derek! Welcome to the neighborhood! I am Arnold and this is my wife Meredith! Next time you come, make a few steps down, and pay us a visit."

"Hi, Meredith and Arnold, we both thank you for your warm welcome and for the invitation! We will come visit you with great pleasure! Bye now!"

He turned toward Ana, put his arms around her shoulders, looked in her eyes, and said:

"Nitti, you are my fiancée since the first moment we've met."

She did not say a word. He continued:

"I will race you to that far bush. Who wins gets a kiss."

He won and she got the kiss. They were famished, sat down on the blanket and enjoyed everything was in the basket. After that, he took her hand and they went for a walk, all the way to the far border. Ana had her camera and took pictures from all corners and sides, making sure not to skip any part that seemed to be interesting.

"Stop it", he said. "Since when are you taking pictures? You never did this before."

"Well, I found that I have a new talent, and a new hobby. Are there wild creatures that might roam around?"

"Bunnies and deer, as far as I know; could be some others. We have plenty of time to find out later."

"How big is this land?" she asked. "If you want to build a house here, it will require a lot of maintenance. It is a safe ground?"

"Almost two acres and needs no maintenance since this is a wilderness area and it should be kept just the way it is with no human interference. Before I bought it, I asked a team of geologists to come up here and inspect every inch of the land. They found it very safe and suitable for building."

That day was very rewarding for both. They could plenty enjoy everything they both liked, in a world of their own, where anything dear to them was possible and which was filled with love and care for each other. Late evening they went home to Derek's place.

The month of April was almost there and Derek's birthday was approaching. One morning, Ana went to the Art Gallery, looked around, and entered the main hall of the sculpture wing. A big exhibit of modern and classic art was in full display to be visible from all corners and sides. She approached a nicely dressed woman sitting at a desk and asked for the Director of the gallery. The woman talked something on the phone, and a short man with white hair, and very courteous manners, probably in his sixties showed up.

"I am Doctor Walter Blum, director of the Art Gallery, at your service, Miss..?"

"My name is Ana Landers. Thank you Doctor Blum for taking time and see me. I would like to commission a small sculpture, about one foot by eight inches, made from these pictures shown like that."

On a table nearby, she put on display in the right sequence, ten pictures taken at the last picnic up there at the Eden place. The short man took from his pocket a magnifier and examined carefully each photo at the time.

"I think we can make something of it. Come tomorrow late afternoon, to look at the design and give me your approval if you like it. The gallery closes at eight. We will discuss material and cost. It was a pleasure to meet you, Miss Landers. Goodbye."

"I will be here around six. Goodbye Doctor Blum."

On her way back home, Ana thought that almost everybody in this world was kind of a Doctor of something. She left herself out of this guild without any regrets. Next day, at six in the afternoon, she was at the gallery, and asked for the nice Doctor Blum. He showed up with a roll of paper in his hands. The design was outstanding, showing most of what was in her photos, with lots of accents for details.

"It's beautiful", Ana said.

"I know it is. We have great artists here, very devoted to their work. Tell me, about material, Miss Landers: would it be plaster, wood, or marble."

She chose marble, not knowing yet how much it will cost.

"The price for marble is higher than for other materials, but I'm sure you can afford it."

When she heard it, her body became softer and softer, but she stood there up straight and strong, displaying a big and charming smile.

"I believe marble is more appropriate. I would like you to make in the back of the border, two small penholders. On the front base, right in the middle, I would like you to write with golden letters the word 'Eden'."

"So will be. The project will be ready in three weeks from today. Here are your photos. The sculptor made a single picture from above for the design."

She signed the contract, made a deposit, and left. On her way back home, she kept talking to herself:

"How am I going to pay for this? It is very expensive, but is an exquisite work of art, with a lot of meaning. I will take some money from my saving account even if this will dry my money quite a bit. He is going to love it, and surely, he is going to ask about the cost. I am not going to tell him, because, I will say, it's a present."

It was not the first time when she was worried, and certainly not the last one. After sorting out her thoughts by moving them back and forth, Ana felt relieved somehow, and with less pressure in her mind. For a few days, Ana and Derek could not see each other because of their busy schedule, and only talked on the phone late in the evening.

One morning Derek called the best video recording studio that he heard abut having a big reputation, and made an appointment for the next day. He woke up early, spent time more than usually to dress up, took his violin, and went to the studio, asking the clerk at the front desk, for the engineer in charge. A tall man in his late forties showed up. Derek told him in details what he wanted: To make a video with music and words, about to an hour long. The engineer escorted him to a room packed with the most modern equipment and gave him all the instructions to follow. They will make a draft first, to count the time for each sequence and to find the right position for each movement. He showed Derek where to sit in front of the camera, asked him to look first in the mirror for the best presentation, and adjusted the headphone over his ears. He went to the other room, which was separated by a glass wall, took the microphone, set his headphone, checked the communication with Derek, and said:

"You can start."

After a few minutes, Derek took his violin and played a piece of music, then stopped and talked in the microphone. He repeated this sequence of playing music alternating with talking, for several times until he finished. In the meantime, the engineer took notes, and was timing every sequence in minutes and seconds with his stopwatch. When Derek gave him a sign that he finished what he had to do, the engineer entered the room and said:

"Let's watch it and see what improvements have to be done."

He made some comments checked Derek's appearance, took off his headphone, showed him the right position, and gave him new instructions how to proceed. He put his notes next to him and said:

"We are going to make the real thing now, and I will be behind the camera. When you play stand up. When you talk sit down. Follow my signals for each sequence, and try to be relaxed. Everything will be fine."

It took them about one hour to finish the video. The engineer looked pleased.

"We are going to play the video, and then I will edit it for the visual image, sound, and synchronization. You can watch my work, or you can come later."

"I will watch", Derek said.

They went to another room that looked like a laboratory. The engineer did what he said, using all kind of complicated tools, magnifiers, sound amplifiers, and apparatuses, working for about one hour. In the meantime, Derek watched without uttering a word. When he finished, the engineer said:

"Let's try it."

It was no less than magnificent. It was even more beautiful than Derek expected. The engineer said:

"I saw maybe thousands of videos made in my studio, but nothing expressing love in such a sublime way. With your permission, may I keep a copy for myself?"

"I will be happy. I do not know how much to thank you. This is more beautiful than I anticipated."

He took his video like a most precious treasure, and went home. In that day, he watched his video repeatedly, without having enough of it.

After a few days, Doctor Blum called Ana:

"Your love land is ready. You can come at anytime to pick it up."

"I will be there tomorrow at six. Thank you for calling, Doctor Blum."

The next day she went to the gàllery. The sculpture was awesome. Made of green, veined marble, it displayed even the smallest details with accuracy and grace.

"It is exquisite", Ana said, "may I have it wrapped up in gift paper?"

"Certainly, and I give you even a big bow," Doctor Blum said.

He called the sculptor and told him what to do. Ana expressed her gratitude to both, took her precious piece of art, and left. At home, she hid it in a corner of a closet until the time will come to give it to Derek for his birthday.

They saw each other after a few days. She asked:

"What plans do you have for celebrating your twenty-fifth? You want us to go somewhere with special meaning?"

"I want us to stay at my home, having a nice dinner, a long talk, and beautiful music, without anyone else around."

"Sounds great. I want the same, and I will prepare everything for dinner while you will set the table and make a pleasant surrounding. Because I do not have time to cook, I will order your favorite dishes and a big chocolate cake. How is that?"

"Splendid. Until then I have a lot of work to do in the field, making some changes to the plans and some adjustments for the construction. All these because of the conditions shown by the terrain. I'll call you."

Ana had a lot of work to do also, in the lab and for her thesis. After a couple of days, she placed the order for dinner, took the sculpture and went to Derek's home around six o'clock. He was waiting for her with a beautifully arranged table and soft music.

"Happy Birthday, Dery", she said when he opened the door. He gave him the package.

"This is quite heavy. I can't imagine what this might be, but I am terribly curious."

He put the package on his desk and opened it. He just stood there with his eyes wide open and agape at the view. He was a fine artist and understood at first sight the high quality of that work.

"Just say something and don't stay there like a piece of rock", Ana said. She loved the expression of his face and enjoyed every second of watching it.

"I don't have words to say how I feel."

"Thank you, Nitti, would be nice."

Derek did not even hear her. He bent over the sculpture moving around it, and checking every detail.

"Even the bush we were racing to, is here. It is a marvelous piece of art. Just awesome. I never dreamed to see something like this, much less to have it to be mine."

Slowly, he came out from his state of ecstasy, took her face in to his hands, and whispered:

"Beyond everything, I treasure your thoughts and feelings you put together for me and gave me such a splendid gift, like a symbol of the place where we will be always happy."

He gave her a long kiss with all his warmth and love. While sitting at the table over the rich dishes, Derek stood up several times to look repeatedly at the sculpture and mumbling:

"Now I know why she took so many pictures. This marvel must cost a fortune. I can't take my eyes of it."

He just fell in love with it.

The following days both were busy with their schedules, and only could talk late night on the phone, before going to sleep. Ana was almost ready with her thesis, her advisor read her paper for the sixth time, and was very satisfied. She will defend it in the beginning of June before the committee, and the date was set one week before her twenty-third birthday. Until then she had to spend a lot of time in the lab, working on the project she was assigned to, and which seemed more complicated with every passing day.

One Sunday they made time to go to their Eden place, and they both asked Ana's parents to drive up there and join them for a picnic. This time Emily prepared the basket with food and beverages. Matthew knew very well the place, while his wife saw it for the first time and was enchanted. Before starting the picnic, Matthew mentioned Derek's birthday, and since they missed it, he gave him an expensive camera as a gift from his and Emily's part. Derek was delighted, saying that besides enjoying it, he will use it a lot to fallow the construction progress of his project in the field. They spent almost the entire day over there, also paying a visit as promised, to their neighbors Meredith and Arnold Jacobson. He was a car dealer and she was a homemaker, both in their fifties, and had two grown up daughters. Their two-story house was nicely furnished, had four bedrooms, a large living room, and a small swimming pool. The hosts gave to all four a warm welcome, with snacks and beverages, hoping to see them soon. They were very pleasant and friendly people. Derek made many pictures and promised to send them. On their way out, going back to their place, he could not abstain himself from making comments:

"The house has many mistakes. It is wrongly oriented, the ceiling is too high, the bedrooms are not in the right place, the kitchen is too small, and all rooms have not enough light. Too bad, because the land is beautiful and they could have built a better structure."

"Is that all?" Ana asked, "I am surprised that you didn't tell them your opinions, and not offered to improve their dwelling, by tearing it down first."

Derek only shrugged his shoulders and said that the house he will build on the Eden place will have no mistakes. Ana knew that and she always recognized that his mind was brilliant. The four of them were already tired from all the excitement during that day, and returned home late in the evening.

The month of May almost ended. Ana finished her thesis of fifty pages and gave it to the members of the committee to read it and prepare their comments. In the beginning of June, the big day for Ana was there to make her presentation and defend her thesis. She entered the room that was indicated to her and took the seat behind a desk that was placed in the middle of it. The members of the committee entered shortly after, and took their seats on a stage, in front of a long desk covered with papers and books. Three of them were members of the faculty, including Ana's advisor, and the fourth one was a scientist from outside the University. After stating their names, one of them addressed Ana, explaining the procedure of the examination that she already knew. The questions started, from simple to most complicate and they kept taking notes, insisting on small details, and making sure that nothing will be overlooked. Ana answered with great confidence to all of them, until the entire atmosphere gradually changed into a field of discussion among scientists with remarkable knowledge. After more than three hours, the member of the committee that seemed to be in charge addressed Ana:

"It was a great pleasure Miss Landers to listen to your defense, and a very interesting experience for the committee to participate in a productive discussion which I am sure, we all enjoyed greatly. Congratulations and best wishes."

They left together, leaving Ana behind still sitting on her chair. She was exhausted.

Outside the building, Derek was waiting for her. She told him everything, not missing any detail and not hiding her big excitement. He was more than happy.

"Let's go eat something and celebrate your success."

They went to their favorite bistro, continuing to talk and sharing their feelings as usually. The next day Ana went to the Institute and was greeted with a round of applauses by her colleagues. She smiled and told them that she was extremely pleased and hoped that they all will have a wonderful collaboration as before. Miss Marple approached her:

"Boss wants to see you."

Ana went upstairs with mixed feelings. Doctor Blake was standing at the window when she entered his office.

"You made quite an impression on my distinguished colleagues. Congratulations for your success. Did you make your decision regarding the doctoral degree?"

"I decided not to enroll in the program, for personal reasons."

"I respect your judgment, even if I do not agree with it. Even so, you will have a full time job with a considerable increase of your salary. Your work is greatly appreciated by the management and by your colleagues, as well."

"Thank you Professor Blake."

It seemed that there was nothing else to add. She went to the door, when he said:

"I am glad to have you here, Ana."

She turned around and whispered, enough loud to be heard by him:

"I am glad to be here, Professor Blake."

Ana returned to her place and worked all day long. There was no need for the time being to spend so many hours in the library. What she had now, will be probably for the rest of her life. She loved her work and acquiring more knowledge every day will give her a great satisfaction in pursuing many rewarding accomplishments. Her schedule was now from eight to four, without flexible hours. Whenever her work will require more research, she will come earlier in the morning to make an uninterrupted development to the project.

Ana's birthday was nearby. A few days before, Derek asked her where she wanted to celebrate it.

"At home, and without any festive decorations", she said "and only on Sunday, since my schedule now is different than before. Probably my parents will want us to be there and join them over dinner, but I rather postpone my birthday celebration for another time. Actually, I do not have any pleasure of it."

It was Friday her birthday, when Derek came in the evening at her door with a bouquet of wild flowers.

"Happy Birthday, my dearest Nitti."

He kissed her with all the warmth of his soul. They went to the living room and gave her a small package, nicely wrapped up in a gift paper, but without a card. She opened it:

"A videotape? What are you up to, now?"

Derek took her by the shoulders, and made her sit on the couch. He turned on the television set, inserted the video in the slot of the player machine, and took his place in the armchair, toward the side. The video started with a first screen showing Ana's pendant at large scale and below it was the word *"Forever"* in gold letters. Schubert's *Serenade* was playing in the background.

Ana opened her mouth to say something but no words came out. The next screen showed Derek with his violin, all dressed up in a black tuxedo playing the *Adagio* from Bruch's violin concerto Nr.1. His face was transfigured and his eyes were like looking into deepness only by him known. In the following screen, Derek was reciting in French from Baudelaire's *Les Fleurs du Mal.* His voice was soft, warm, and full of love.

Ana had tears in her eyes, flowing down on her cheeks, without her bothering to wipe them. He was watching her from aside, feeling an immense joy. The next screen showed Derek playing the solo violin from *Scheherazade* followed by him reciting from the poems of *Lamartine.* Ana was overwhelmed with a powerful feeling of wonder, without being able to make a move. In the following screen, Derek was playing Beethoven's *Violin Romance,* showing a tremendous emotional feeling. His next appearance was in reciting from Verlaine's *symbolist Poems.* His voice had languishing tones like uncovering a sentimental melancholy. The atmosphere became different with the next screen where he played the first movement from Tchaikovsky's

Violin Concerto. His emotional tone expressed in verses changed into a passionately intonation of love revealed through his music. In the next screen, Derek recited from Pierre Ronsard's *Les Amours.* His voice was whispering with softer tones for each verse, like a prelude to the next screen in which he played Schubert's *Ave Maria.*

The last screen showed Derek with deep emotion expressed on his face. His voice in English this time was like a trembling whisper:

"The human soul is created with intricate patterns that no one ever knew in the past, and most certain, no one will ever know in the future how deep their meanders are. You touched an intense chord mysteriously veiled in my soul that not even I knew it existed there. I look into your worshiped eyes and see the light of my life. I take you into my arms and keep you close to my soul, touching your warm feelings with my tender emotion, and having a vision of the shiny stars above, smiling over us, my dearly beloved Nitti, now and…

Below appeared the word "*Forever*" in gold letters, like in the first screen.

Everything became quiet. Ana had her face covered with both hands, not being able to move. She cried. He put his arms around her shoulders, keeping her close, and not uttering a word. It took her a while until she came to her senses.

"Why are you giving me suffering instead of joy?" she asked.

"They both go together, side by side, and touch the same chord. All depends on the stimulus that is triggered by the mind and is activated first."

"I will not watch this video again for a long time, until I will reach the level of your emotional sensibility, if ever I will be able to stretch my perceptions to the extent of your effusive state of mind."

After three weeks, they were married. The small wedding ceremony was held at the Landers' house and only a few friends were invited to participate in that special event.

Ana moved to Derek's place, taking with her only what she considered to be necessary. The rest was given to charity. In the first couple of days both were enjoying a lot the adjustments for living together and could not have enough of the happy atmosphere filled with talking, laughing, joking, and kissing every time they were stumbling into each other.

They both had the same schedule at work and came home at the same time. In the kitchen, while telling each other about their day, both prepared dinner competing for the best-cooked dishes, since there was no longer need for ordering food like before. They loved being married. Both were very young, healthy, had a comfortable home, good, and very well paid jobs, and a long life ahead to be happy. Most of all, they adored each other.

Time went by and the month of August was already there. One day Derek asked:

"Remember our plan to go on vacation? Remember that we decided to go to the Belize? I think that we should do it now. I have two weeks vacation coming and I believe you can arrange for yours. We can afford even a luxury trip and have a leisure time enjoying the fresh air of the Caribbean Sea. It will be our honeymoon."

"I would love us to go. Let me talk to the management about my vacation schedule. I know that I am entitled to only two weeks, but these will be plenty of time for the trip."

Derek went to the travel agency and booked a round trip to Belize for the coming week. Rent car, and tour guided trips to see the most attractive sites were included in the price for a luxury room at a hotel not far from the beach. They flew to Belize City, and at the airport, the rented car was waiting for them. Four kilometers they had to drive to the hotel which was a charming Bed and Breakfast establishment located in a safe, quiet residential area only a block far from the beautiful Caribbean Sea. The room was spacious, very clean, and comfortable. Both Ana and Derek were extremely pleased and decided to get the most of their vacation and not wasting any precious time. In the same day, they visited the surroundings, took a walk on the seashore, and had dinner at a restaurant where the owners, a very friendly couple, served local food. The next day was scheduled for a guided tour to the cayes and atolls, the small low islands composed of sand and coral fragments. The view was exquisite and the tour guide gave them many indications about the geologic features of those places. Many taken photos by both of them will be greatly cherished when they will return home. In the coming days, a tour was scheduled to visit the "Altun Ha Maya Ruins", departing from Belize City and riding along the Caribbean Sea. The way was going toward the dense jungle surrounding the archeological site of the Maya ruin and the scenic views of the jungle was breath taking. The guide was very knowledgeable and explained about the Mayan powerful civilization ruling that region, millennia ago. He also illustrated Mayan's religious beliefs, complex calendar development, and advanced writing system. The "Temple of the Masonry Altars" and the "Sun God Tomb" displayed the most impressive architecture. Derek took pictures from all sites and corners, making sure that no details were missing.

Back at the hotel, they talked a lot changing impressions about the many splendors they discovered. Such a fulfilling reward was hard to receive very often. The next few days were spent on the beach, and driving around, visiting the village where many boutiques offered souvenirs at inexpensive prices. They bought some to keep and some to be given to Ana's parents. The last tour was taken to Belize Zoo and Tropical Education Center where they learned about a wide variety of wild animals living in their natural habitats, and the conservation efforts made by the authorities to preserve and protect their environments.

The last day of vacation was there and they flew back home, taking with them many splendid memories of a time never to forget.

One evening Derek came home with many rolled papers specially for making sketches and architectural layouts, and displayed them on his desk.

"Guess what?" he addressed Ana.

"Surprise me."

"I will start the design of our house up there on our Eden land. I have to work at home whenever I can in the afternoon. It will take me quite a bit of time, but I enjoy a lot doing it. Will you join me in making suggestions for a first draft? What do you think?"

"I am all delighted and cannot wait to see the plans. If you ask me I will be happy to come up with my opinions and share with you my humble knowledge about design."

It took him a few days to sketch a rough drawing with many notes written all over the paper. He asked Ana to come over and take a look. She took a seat next to him, impatiently waiting for his explanations.

"This is a preliminary concept. Here is the entrance to the main hall, where you can see a winding stair on each side. The study rooms, yours and mine, are on the right and left side of the hall, and the living room is facing the main door. Next to it is the music room and on the far side is the dining room, a large kitchen and two bathrooms. On the other side, facing a large deck is the gym room. Upstairs are six rooms and four bathrooms, and a small kitchenette for late night snacks. An open deck is extending from three sides of the house. On top is the attic where many unused things can be stored. What do you think?"

Ana looked at him with amazement.

"We do not need all these. Who is going to live there? We need a nice, comfortable home to feel close to each other, live like a family, and raise our children with modesty and decency. This is beyond my comprehension."

"This is the palace I promised you. There will be no children. I will never share you with anyone, and there will be no one between us. It will always be just you and me."

Ana felt like a heavy brick was dropped on her head. She went to the living room, sat on the couch, and tried to put her broken thoughts together. How many of his hidden features are still for her to unveil? She remembered her Psychology professor from college. Her name was Kellie Benton, she was in her fifties, and made a strong impression on Ana's intellect. One day she said:

"The mind has the same design for every human being. Its activation on which way to take is everyone's choice. On the straight path forward, it works usually for normal, average people who perform their duties to their families, and are the backbone of the society. Towards the right path, it works for people ready to make sacrifices for their faith, for their families, or for a cause. Towards the left path, it works for those who lie, steal, blackmail, and prove an unstable behavior.

The upward path is the stream of those in search for excellence and reaches the brilliance of their minds. The downward path goes all the way to the dungeons where evil resides. It takes only one spark to ignite a short circuit that shuts off all the doors to the ways above, and triggers the mechanism of violence, followed by crimes, murders, and mass killings."

Remembering those words, Ana tried to find the correct response to the question she asked herself about the way chosen by Derek to work his mind. She was afraid of the worst. After a couple of hours, he showed up and sat next to her, taking her hand and kissing it:

"I am very sorry Nitti, if I caused you sadness. I did not mean to upset you. I will revise the sketches and resize the house to a smaller scale, making it cozy and comfortable the way you like. Can you forgive me?"

Ana thought hoping for his sake, that maybe he made a blunder when he mentioned that there will be no children.

"Yes, I can forgive you but remember always, and try never to forget that we are not each other's property, meaning that I do not own you, and you do not own me. If you think otherwise, better say it now, and we will have to reconsider our relationship."

He opened his mouth to let out a feeling of anger, which she could sense, but chose a soft voice instead, and said:

"I promise to behave and try not to ever upset you. I will work on the plans and show you the changes. Can we have dinner now?"

She made dinner and they both tried to improve the tense atmosphere, which they never experienced before. After a few days, he showed her the new plans for the house, which this time was much smaller, with only three bedrooms, one staircase, and some amenities, which were necessary to a comfortable household. A small swimming pool on the side made a very pleasant display of the entire area.

"This is much better, and I like it a lot. Thank you for understanding my point of view and I hope that you agree with it. My question is, how are we going to pay for it since we are now paying for the land?"

"I will ask for a loan at the bank, and we will be able to pay for both, the land and the house, without any hardship. I am glad that you like the plans. Maybe in a month or so, I will be ready with the design and we can start to build it. My friend Willie Reiss will help with the construction and the crew, giving me a good deal that we can afford."

Slowly their life together took its former shape, without any emotional disturbance. As always before, they shared thoughts, feelings, and needs, trusting and loving each other.

After about two months, all the arrangements for building the house were made, and the construction started. Both Ana and Derek were highly excited by that endeavor and followed closely every single step of the progress on the construction site. Ana met his friend Willie and she thought he was a very pleasant person, in spite the fact that he was always very distant. Derek went there more often to make sure that everything was carried out according to the design, especially paying attention to the smallest details.

After eight months, the house was finished. As a present for their marriage, even if past due, Ana's parents bought the entire furniture, and everything was essential for the kitchen. Both Ana and Derek were ecstatic when they spent the first weekend in their new home. It was indeed a beautiful place to live in comfort, far from the outside world, and where worries and problems could be totally forgotten. For the time being, they decided to keep their home down the hills, since it was closer to their working places.

The time for vacation was already there, when Derek came up with a proposal:

"How would you like us to go overseas and visit my grandparents in Heidelberg?"

"I'll be delighted to meet them and have a good time together in the place where you were born and grew up. It will be a great pleasure for me to go there."

In the next week, they took a night flight to Heidelberg and arrived in the morning at their destination where Derek's grandparents Anton and Charlotte Weber waited for them at the airport. He was quite a tall man, good looking, wearing glasses, and his hair was all white. She was a beautiful woman, much shorter than her husband, very well dressed, with big blue eyes and white, cut short hair. They both were smiling when they saw the couple coming. Derek rushed into their open arms embracing both of them for a few seconds, and then he said:

"This is Ana, my wife" and, "these are my grandparents, Charlotte and Anton."

"Welcome Ana to our family. You are even more beautiful than Derek described you in his letters," his grandmother said in good English with accent.

"Thank you kindly, Mrs. Weber, I am very pleased to meet and know you and doctor Weber", Ana replied to the friendly greeting.

"Please call us Oma and Opa, short for grandmother and grandfather, just like Derek does."

They looked for their luggage, picked them up, and followed the Webers to the car. After about half hour of driving they arrived at the final destination, the Webers'residence, on the north side of Neckar River. It was a big two-story house in Historicist style originated by both, Romanticism and Classicism. The front doors were carved oak with beveled glass and opened into a hall with an elegant staircase made of chestnut and with a crystal chandelier hanging from the high ceiling. The room to the right of the staircase was Doctor's Weber's office, and next to it was the waiting room for his patients. On the left side was a living room with fireplace, furnished with great taste. Next to it was the music room with mantled fireplace, and where all of the woodwork was oak. All the way back to the hall, a double door was leading to the dining area and kitchen. At the top of the stairs was a family sitting area surrounded by four bedrooms, with opening doors to the deck outside, and each with its own bathroom.

Ana took Derek's hand while he gave her the tour of the house. Everything there was impressive and at a larger scale than she was used to. His grandparents kept Derek's room just the way it was when he left Heidelberg. Ana looked around with wonder at all those rooms decorated with great taste, but nowhere in that big house could she see a single photo of Derek's parents. She was asking herself many questions, but was not brave enough to speak up loud in front of Derek or his grandparents. Maybe when the right time will come, she will find out the answer to that puzzle. The housekeeper in her late sixties, by the name Gretchen, who served in the family since Derek was born, took their luggage, showed them to the guestroom, and said that lunch will be served at twelve o'clock.

The diner area was elegantly furnished and the front wall was all glass with one door opening to a large veranda. The four of them talked a lot over a delicious lunch, mostly German cuisine, after which they moved to the living room where coffee and beverages were served, continuing to recollect the time passed since Derek's last visit. Ana was tired and wished to take a nap, but she was not in the position to express her feelings. Sometimes they spoke German, and she felt like an outsider because she did not understand the language and could not participate in the conversation. Finally, Derek asked her if she wanted to go for a short walk to see the neighborhood. It was late afternoon, the fresh air outside made her feel better and she was glad to become more relaxed. The streets were narrow without any traffic and people strolled along the Neckar River bank. Heidelberg is renowned for its romantic ambiance and is an endlessly walkable little city. Ana liked mostly the scale of everything she saw, thinking that people there knew better to adjust their lives to a more balanced size of what usually makes beauty and comfort to be highly valued.

Late evening they returned to the Weber's house, changed a few words with the hosts, went to bed, and slept all night without moving. They both were exhausted after too much excitement for one day. The next few days were spent around the city visiting many historic monuments and sites in the Old Town, such as the Old Bridge with a gate and two towers, the Heidelberg University and its Library, The Church of the Holy Spirit, the baroque-styled buildings on the main shopping street.

Both Ana and Derek enjoyed being together, talking about the places they visited which were well known by Derek and totally new for Ana.

By the end of the week, Anton asked Derek to accompany him for a drive to Frankfurt to visit his brother Klaus who was very ill. He addressed Ana:

"It is not a pleasant trip, my dear girl, and I am suggesting that you should stay home with Charlotte. I am sure that you both will have plenty to do for entertaining each other. We will be back on Monday morning."

Ana was elated, but did not show any expression on her face. The time for solving the big puzzle in Derek's life was there, and she will take this big opportunity to find out the answer.

"Certainly, Opa. Have a safe trip and please give my regards and best wishes to uncle Klaus. I will walk you to the car."

She walked with them outside, smiled and gave them a kiss, returned to the house, went to the study, took a book and sitting comfortable in an armchair started reading. She was prepared for a long conversation when she heard Charlotte's voice:

"Here you are, my dear. What would you like us to do? Maybe we can go shopping and you will see the charming boutiques we have, with many goodies to choose from and buy. What do you say?"

"I will be delighted, Oma. Please allow me to ask first, why there is no picture of Derek's parents in the entire house?"

Charlotte sighed, came close to the other armchair, and sat down.

"There are plenty, but I took them away for Derek's sake, just to avoid him to remember. I assume that he never told you about the tragedy that struck our family when he was a little child. Now that you are a member of our family, I think that you have to know."

"He only told me that his parents died in a plane crash when he was about six years of age. I never asked questions because I understood that he avoided touching that subject, and I always respected his privacy."

"As I said, you should know. It was the month of January that year when Derek was not even six years old. Louise and Ethan took a vacation to Zermatt in Switzerland because they both loved skiing. One night, Derek started coughing and had high fever. Anton and I rushed him to the hospital and he was diagnosed with pneumonia. The doctor said not to worry to much because with the right medication and care he will be all right in a few days. Even so, we thought that it was our responsibility to call his parents and let them know. They both were worried so much about the child, that they chartered a small plane to make the trip shorter and to be home sooner. It was a big snow storm in that area, the plane crashed over the mountains, and their bodies were never found."

Charlotte took a long pause, sighed, and continued:

"A few days later, Derek was healthy enough to come home from the hospital. He asked about his parents and we told him that they were still on vacation. We had no idea how to tell him the truth. Since he was at the age to understand, both Louise and Ethan taught him never to lie, never to hide from the truth, and be responsible for everything he does. Anton and I thought that it was better to tell him, since sooner or later, he will find out and then his response might be worse. Therefore, we told him the truth, and we were horrified by his reaction. He did not show a sign of grief or tears; instead, he became mute and was incapable to move. The shock was too big and heavy for him.

She took a deep breath, made again a pause, and continued:

"Time passed by, we took him to a renown psychiatrist specialized in children therapy, who told us Derek suffered a trauma, his mind was completely blocked, and maybe in good time he will slowly recover; but a circuit in his brain will be always there to react unpredictably at the smallest bit of awareness regarding that terrible tragedy. After a couple of months, he started making some sounds and trying to utter some words. With great difficulty he could articulate either in French or German: "maman et papa sont morts à cause de moi", and "Mama und Papa haben wegen mir gestorben". He kept repeating over and over again only these sentences. As you can see Ana, his entire childhood was darkened by that tragedy. He never touches that subject, never talks about his parents, and never shares his intimate feelings regarding them. What is in his mind no one knows. He adored his parents, especially his mother, who used to take him to the park, play with him, making him laugh, and telling him bed time stories every night before he went to sleep. I will show you the pictures of my daughter and her husband. They adored each other, and both adored Derek. Louise had a small fashion boutique not far from here, and Ethan was an Architect."

With very slow movements she went to the desk and took from a drawer a few photos showing them to Ana. They both were very good looking, but Louise was exquisetely beautiful. Derek took from both his handsome features, his smile, the expression in his eyes. Ana was overwhelmed with strong emotions by listening to that tragic story and by looking at the photos of those beautiful people who were Derek's parents. She was trembling when she said:

"I am totally shocked by everything you told me. My words are not enough to express my sadness, and I cannot even imagine the terrible time you all had. I only can think that you, Opa, and especially Derek need lot of courage to live everyday trying to cover the deep pain, which will always be in your souls. Thank you Oma for trusting me and sharing with me such a tremendous suffering you all have been through."

She approached Charlotte, embraced, and kissed her with great warmth. Charlotte looked in Ana's eyes and whispered:

"By that time, his doctor also told us that sometime later in his life, the guilt deeply buried in his soul might burst out in a terrible rage and then nobody will be able to control him, or do something to alleviate his pain. It might not happen, the doctor said, all depending on his day-by-day frame of mind. I know, my dear girl that you love him very much, but watch your steps and be careful. He might become dangerous."

Ana was terrified but said nothing. She will think how to handle an unpredictable situation if it will occur. They both went shopping, trying to change that emotional atmosphere into a tolerable disposition.

Anton and Derek returned from their trip, both looking tired and without much willingness to make conversation. Uncle Klaus was ill but in good spirit, they said. Late that evening, before going to bed, Derek took Ana by the shoulders, forced her to look in his eyes, and said:

"She told you."

Ana caressed his face with affection, showing a mixture of compassion and love, making sure that he will understand her emotions.

"Yes, she told me. Let us not talking about this, now or ever, unless you feel like sharing with me your susceptibility in this regard, and give me the opportunity to express my thoughts."

He took her in his arms and kissed her with love. She understood that the subject was closed and he will never talk about it. In a way, Ana felt a sensation of relief, and decided to respect his feelings and his privacy as she always did.

The time for returning home was there. It was an affectionate reveal of leaving each others, after promising to stay in touch and writing long letters about their daily lives.

In their cozy home they felt relaxed after that vacation marked with enjoyable and sad experiences, each kept as a distinct recollection for a long time. Derek's birthday was nearby and Ana was thinking about a present with a special meaning for him, when he said:

"Let us not exchange presents for out birthdays anymore. You are my present and I am yours, always. Do you agree?"

Every time he touched that sensitive subject about "ownership" regarding them, Ana was shivering. The warning words of Charlotte were like a needle in her brain, and caution was always there to remind her about the next move she had to make.

"Sounds good to me. I was thinking that we should have a party up there to Eden, not necessarily for your birthday, but just for having a good time, with our neighbors and our friends. What do you think?"

"Great idea! Let us plan it and send some invitations. We can cater for the party, since we do not have time to spare for shopping and cooking. I can't wait to dance with you!"

Lots of guests came over, sharing a great time, good food, music, dancing, and the friendly company of their charming hosts. The party was a real success, and both Ana and Derek were extremely pleased, knowing that every one of their guests had a feeling of big contentment.

Next day they went back home down the hills returning to their daily routine. Both had a lot of work to do and saw each other only in the evening when they talked a lot about their projects, colleagues, and some gossips going around. One day, Derek told her that Willie gave him two tickets to the Opera because he and his wife could not go.

"What is playing?" Ana asked.

"Lohengrin, with a great cast."

"Let's go then", she said, even if she only liked Wagner's overtures, and nothing else of his opera music. They had a big selection of videos and classic music, and every time they had the chance to go to the music store, they bought different interpretations of the same pieces. Both Ana and Derek grew up in a surrounding where music was essential to their mode of living, and therefore it was natural for them to become educated and knowledgeable in that particular field. Ana started long ago to make a classified inventory on her computer, but never had time enough to do more than very little.

The next day was raining and Derek had to go the construction site for his new project. He caught a mild cold, had a little fever, was coughing, and complaining about his poor condition. Ana told him to stay home, try to relax, gave him medication, and said:

"Behave like a man, and not like a spoilt little boy. I'll be back before you know it."

Derek's eyes suddenly darkened, his face was like dazed, and Ana sensed a menace. He just remembered that those were the last words of his mother when he saw her for the last time, and she never came back. With a stern voice, he asked:

"Do you still love me?"

"Yes, my dearest, I love you a lot."

The look in his eyes changed to a warm expression and his features became animated by joy. Ana went to work carrying in her mind a shadow of discontent but tried to put it aside for the time being.

He called her after one hour and Miss Marple approached her:

"Derek said that he is very sick and wants you to come home."

"He is not very sick at all. He has only a mild cold but likes to play mama's little boy. If he calls again, please Miss Marple, tell him to behave and I will bring him chocolate candies."

"You two are some lovers I have never seen before", Miss Marple said with a big smile.

Ana came home after work, he tried to impress her with his state of health, but she knew already that he was in a very good shape and could go to work the next day.

"I want us both to stay home tomorrow and you take care of me because I am still sick".

"You wish. You are not sick at all and you go to work like a good, responsible person. Your fever is gone and so is your cough. You are in a very good condition and try to behave like a normal human being."

He mumbled with disappointment but he knew that she was right, as most of the time.

It was the beginning of August already, with warm weather and lots of sunshine. Every weekend they went up hill to Eden, enjoying their wonderful house and land. It was a beautiful night with full moon, clear sky and trillions of stars above. They went swimming like so many times before, racing each other along the pool, and having a marvelous time. Derek looked at Ana and said:

"You have the body of an awesomely beautiful Greek goddess sculptured in marble."

"And you have the body of a Greek warrior, extremely handsome and attractive."

"Now that we established our Greek ancestry, I shall dress you in a robe made of celestial stars, raise you on a pedestal, and will protect you with eternal faithfulness from every one daring to take you away from me."

Ana's head started spinning and she felt that needle in her brain reminding her about Oma's words every time Derek touched that subject of possessing her like his right to a ownership. She made no more comments because she wanted him not to continue with that topic that always made her envisaging a shaky ground.

After a couple of months, they received a long letter from Oma, saying that Anton died from complications of pneumonia. Derek took a few days off and flew to Heidelberg for the funerals, alone, since Ana could not leave her project that had a pressing due date. Being alone for the first time, Ana asked herself how would be her life without Derek. She missed him a lot and thought that she will never be able to fulfill her existence without him. She fell in love with him long ago and nothing changed in her feelings for him ever since. When he returned, they both rushed into each other's arms like if they were apart for a very long time.

One night before going to sleep, Ana said:

"Maybe it would be better for us to move full time up there to Eden. It is useless to keep this place when we have there such a beautiful house, and besides, we can save a lot of money. A half hour or maybe a little more of driving to our jobs, will not make a big difference. What do you think?"

"I think that this is an excellent idea, and I love it. Next week we start packing and I will take care of all the arrangements."

The following week they were ready to move out and go to their place called Eden that was indeed the terrestrial paradise. It took them quite a bit of time to rearrange the furniture, make room for more books and more music, find the better spots for working their papers, and making a jewel of their kitchen. After a couple of days, the house looked more beautiful than they expected.

With a considerable amount of money left to him by his grandfather, Derek opened his own office in the most expensive area in the center of the city, and took his good friend Willie Reiss as a partner. They hired a few young architects and designers and shortly after, the firm flourished vigorously. Time for a long vacation was not anymore possible to be reached, since being the boss now, Derek had many more other responsibilities than before and could not have the luxury to take any time off. After a while, the reputation of his firm spread along the city to a broad extent, and rich people commissioned him to build their expensive houses. Many times Derek had to stay until late night to do his work, and saw Ana only when he came home and she was already asleep. On a tray in the dining room, a hearty dinner was waiting for him, but he was so tired that barely touched it. He went to bed, took her in his arms, kissing her and saying:

"Good night Nitti."

Ana heard him like in a dream, and before she wished him good night, Derek was already asleep.

One day she suggested him to hire more people, because he is getting tired with every passing day. Derek followed her advice, hired two more architects with big experience and three more designers to help Willie with the construction. It was a very wise decision he made, and his working schedule came gradually to a more convenient tempo.

Ana and Derek had the best of their life, enjoying every minute of being together, treasuring their happiness, and being in love like never before.

Time went by, another year passed with every day leaving behind precious memories never to be forgotten. By the end of October they celebrated one year since they moved to Eden. A big party with friends, colleagues, and neighbors took place in a cheering atmosphere where every one had a tremendous time.

Shortly after, Ana's father, Matthew died of a heart attack. Ana was overwhelmed with grief, since he was always her friend and a role model, from whom she learned the many aspects of decency, fairness, and dignity, which became the foundation of her character. Both Ana and Derek went to the funerals, attended by many of Matthew's and Emily's friends and colleagues who admired and highly respected them.

Ana stayed with her mother for a couple of days, trying without any success to comfort her. She and Matt were everything to each other after Ana left their home. They shared together many years of a marriage that was made like in heavens. Now, Emily was alone in a big house filled with memories left by both, her daughter and her husband. She told Ana that her work at the hospital will be her only comfort, to bring quietude to her patients and ease their pain. Friends of the family, she said, will be always there for her, giving her the feeling that she was not alone. Besides, she added, sometime she and Matt will be reunited and be happy again forever. Ana was not sure about that statement, but she highly respected her mother's belief, especially in those moments of her big suffering.

Ana returned home taking with her the beloved images of her parents. Derek was all the time around her, comforting her and surrounding her with his love. Slowly, everything came back on the right path of a normal course of life, leaving Ana with a deep sadness that she will always carry in her soul. Her father left her quite a big sum of money, and Ana opened a new account in her name, thinking that later she might buy something expensive for Derek, and maybe for her too.

Christmas was already there. They decided to spend it alone, just the two of them, since all their friends and colleagues had their own families to be with, and Emily has to work without celebrating the holidays. A small tree with decorations was in the living room and some symbolic presents for each other, they put underneath. The next day was snowing with big flakes covering the land with a beautiful white mantle, when they took a walk, playing, racing each other, and having a wonderful time.

The New Year's Eve came by and this time Emily joined them for the celebration. They had dinner in front of the fireplace, recollecting the good times spent together in the past years. Back at work, every one was busy with schedules, plans, projects, and tasks to be fulfilled in due time. One day by the end of January, Derek told Ana, when both were sitting by the fireplace:

"I was thinking how fortunate we are. We have everything one could dream of. We are young, healthy, have good working places, a wonderful house, and most of all we love each other, like always before. Every time I look at you, I tell myself that I never have enough of you, that much I adore you."

Ana took a big breath before saying:

"You will have more than enough of me. I am pregnant."

His face became livid, his eyes darkened, and his body was trembling.

"You will have an abortion. I know a good clinic and the doctor is a friend of Willie. There will be no children between us. I told you before that I will not share you with anybody in the world. I will not let anybody to take your love for me and that is only mine."

Ana looked at him with horror. She felt a heavy brick was dropped on her head again like the first time he made the same shocking confession. Looking straight in his eyes, she said with a resolute tone:

"I will not have an abortion. My love for you will never be taken or shared. It is a big difference between the love I have for you and the love for my children. Can you not know and understand at least this much?"

"What I know and understand is exactly what I said: You will have an abortion. I told you once before, and I am telling you again, that it will always be just you and me. Remember what I told you some time ago, that you are my goddess that I dressed in a robe made of celestial stars, raised you on a pedestal, and I am your warrior that protects you with eternal faithfulness from every one daring to take you away from me."

His voice was full of sarcasm with a sound of a snicker when he added:

"Or perhaps you prefer to have a miscarriage!"

He turned around and left. Ana felt like she broke into pieces. For a while, she was unable to put her thoughts together and think straight. She just sat there, crushed on the couch and only staring at the wall before her eyes. Where to go and ask for help? She had no intimate friends to share with them the inmost depths of her life. If she told her mother, Emily will become furious and show Derek her anger, which will make everything to be worse. Ana remembered Kellie Benton, her professor of Psychology, and her lecture about the human mind when she mentioned ... "The downward path goes all the way to the dungeons where evil resides". She decided to call and make an appointment. The next day Ana took time off and went to meet her professor. She told her everything since the beginning not omitting any detail she considered important. The Doctor listened without interrupting her and took many notes. When Ana finished her long exposure of her critical situation, they both took a long pause, and the Doctor started her analysis:

"Ana, my dear, you are in a very intricate situation, which requires a very careful approach in every step you make. Derek is a very sick man. When he lost his mother at that tender age, he suffered a big trauma, which was not properly treated at that time, which therefore never healed, and because of that, the pain he suffered was deeply buried in his mind. The reason for the progress of his condition was not only the loss of his mother but the way he punished himself with the burden of guilt, considering himself the only cause of his mother's death, from which he never recovered. Ever since, he tried to find the love that meant everything for him, made him feel alive and happy. When he met you and started to know you, his longtime concealed feelings were resurrected and became stronger with every passing day. For him love has no distinction, as if it is for any normal human being. He cannot recognize the difference between the particular feeling of love given by a mother to her children, and the emotional state of love given to a husband, and even the feeling of warmth given to a dear friend. For Derek love means the intense passion for someone whom he considers his property owned only by him. Whenever he senses a threat, his emotional state reaches the highest altitude of action and becomes out of control. Passion is the strongest feeling a human can have, has the same power in love as in hate, and when is merged with obsession, it becomes the most unfailing destine of destruction."

The Doctor made a pause, and looked at Ana who was no less than a pitiful woman completely helpless. With a very soft voice she continued:

"For anyone in his entourage, Derek looks like a perfectly normal person, pleasant, friendly, and charming. Even a psychiatrist doctor, will not be able to analyze his mind, since he will never disclose what is deeply buried in the "dungeons of his soul, where evil resides". He is capable of doing anything drastic to preserve what he considers belonging only to him and cannot be shared with anyone, even with his own child. Ana, my dear girl, I only advise you to be extremely careful, because you are in danger. He will never let you go, and be sure, he will find you anywhere you will try to hide. I suggest having your mother moving with you, if you want to have your child, and be ready to call the authorities in case his condition gets worse. I am here for you, anytime, day or night, and you can come to me always without any appointment."

"I do not know how to thank you, Doctor Benton for enlighten me with your knowledge about what was so confused and hard for me to understand. At least, I can think more clearly even if I do not know what will be my next step for the time being."

They embraced each other and the doctor said:

"Please call me Kellie, and consider me as a good friend. Good bye Ana and take care of you."

"Thank you again, my good friend Kellie. Good bye."

On her way home, Ana tried to put her thoughts together to find the right solution for dealing with Derek's tendency to break her soul and her life. She was firmly determined to fight him until the last drop of her breath, or his.

Derek was home, waiting for her with a very offensive welcome:

"I called you at work and Miss Marple said that you took the day off. Where have you been?"

This time her voice was full of sarcasm with a sound of a snicker when she answered:

"I looked for a clinic to have an abortion but could not find any, since abortion is prohibited by law."

Derek came close to her and slapped her in the face so hard that blood sprang from her nose, flowing down her blouse. Ana did not make a move, but his face was terrified. He stretched his hands to touch her face, when she stepped back. He kneeled and embraced her feet, and his voice was like bursting into tears:

"Please Nitti, I beg your forgiveness. I do not know what occurred to me. I am terribly sorry, please forgive me. It will never happen again, I promise. Can you forgive me?"

Ana looked at him with distaste and only said:

"Let me clean up and then I will make dinner."

The next few days passed without incident, but the harmony that has always been the basic of their relationship, was broken with very little chance to be restored. Ana was convinced that Derek was not giving up on his determination to persuade her to have an abortion, and she was resolute to fight him against any of his intention to harm her. She was careful and watched her every step and when he was home, she kept her phone in the pocket with her finger touching the button of the emergency call. Derek even tried several times to make her stumbling on pieces of furniture that he put in her way, with the intention to make her fall and have a miscarriage. He even spilled on the kitchen floor drops of oil to make her miss her step and slip over the perilous surface. Ana was all the time on full alert, observed every single sneaky scheme he used to harm her, but kept quiet and avoided any discussion that only could have made everything worse. She already accepted with big sadness that he was a sick man, and there was no way for him to be cured. Her dearly beloved Dery was gone forever. One day he tried a different approach, using a cunning tone:

"Since you persist in your stubbornness and do not want to have an abortion, you can give birth and we will put the child for adoption. I am sure we will find a good family to raise him properly and give him everything he needs. Is this more acceptable?"

Ana looked at him with pity and disgust when she answered:

"My Creator gave me the right to be a mother, and neither you nor anyone else will take this right from me. There will be no adoption for my child."

Derek became furiously angry, pushed her with an intense force, Ana fell on her back, and he began yelling like mad:

"Your Creator is not here to confirm your right, but I am here to decide what rights you have!"

He started kicking her trying to reach her womb with his feet. She turned her back up covering her abdomen, and in the same time, she reached her phone in her pocket and pressed the button for emergency. Her called was traced to the address and the ambulance came in few minutes. Derek told the paramedics that Ana stumbled on a chair and fell down. She was rushed to the hospital; the doctor checked carefully her body and found no harm. He mentioned the bruises on her back and legs, and Ana said that she fell, but did not hear his comments. The doctor also made a sonogram and said:

"Guess what? We have twins! Boy and girl, fraternal twins!"

Ana was about to explode of joy. She looked at the picture, the doctor explained her everything with minute details and told her to eat properly and exercise.

Time went by, with increasing tension between Ana and Derek. She kept being extremely careful with every single step she made, avoiding any controversial discussion with him, and trying to make the best she could of that difficult situation. By the end of September, precisely on the twenty-second of the month Ana gave birth to Elise and Andrew the most beautiful fraternal twins one could ever imagine. Their features were taken from both parents, Elise looking more like Derek and Andrew more like Ana. Emily stayed all the time with her daughter at the hospital during her labor and the day after. Ana could no longer hide from her mother the situation in her marriage, and told her almost everything in a smooth way such as not to shock Emily, but enough to make her very upset.

"I am really very sad, and never expected Derek to be otherwise than a very good husband and father. What are you going to do?"

"The Institute where I work has a maternity leave as part of its benefit program and I took one month off in addition to my two weeks regular vacation time, and two weeks leave without pay, to stay home with my babies. I have no idea what will be next for me to do. I might look for a highly skilled nurse with big experience to take her in and take care for the twins. Do you have another suggestion?"

"It so happens that one of my good friends, who is about my age, retired a few months ago, and wants to open her private practice. She is an excellent nurse that worked with children her entire life, and I am sure she will take the job. I know that she lives alone and she will be happy to work for you. I will talk to her and see if she agrees."

After a couple of days, Emily came over and took Ana and the twins, driving them home. Derek was not there and that was a relief for them. The nursery was arranged much before, with everything to provide the twins with the best living conditions for growing healthy and happy. Ana asked her mother to stay over night, just in case Derek will try to make a dramatic scene. He came late in a bad mood, but said nothing in front of Emily. Over dinner, a casual conversation, ignoring the subject regarding the twins, was enough to preserve a calm atmosphere. The next day was Sunday, Emily went home, and Ana made a last attempt. She looked Derek in his eyes, took his face in her hands, and said:

"I love you, Dery. Do not forget ever that I love you. However, I love also our children. We all are a marvelous family, and we all need each other. Please, I beg you, try to change your feelings and be close to the babies and me. Try to understand that we are not anymore just you and me, but we have two children that are part of us and we are part of them. Come, have a look at them, and give them some of your love, no matter how little."

Derek looked at her as if he had nobody before his eyes. She took his hand, and drew him to the nursery, asking him to look at the twins. They were both awake and smiling, moving up and down their little hands. Derek looked at them with disdain and said:

"I do not want them in my life. I will not let them steal what is mine and that is your love for me. I will not let them or anyone else to intrude into our life. They will be put up for adoption. I have already contacted an agency. I hate them!"

He turned his back, and left for the entire day. Ana had not anymore the feeling of being dazed and crushed.

On the contrary, she had a state of consciousness bringing to awareness her strength that was coming to her mind and body. She went to the nursery, and kneeled between the cribs, looking by turn to Elise and Andrew. Keeping her hands like in a prayer, she said:

"Before my Creator and before you, my children, I swear to protect your lives with my life and with my love, for as long as I live. I swear to fight anyone who will try to harm or hurt you, or be a danger for you. I shall raise you over my shoulders and take care of you, with everything in my power to give you all you need to grow up with decency, fairness, and with love and compassion. I beg my Creator to bless with His Grace this oath I took before Him and before you."

She stood up, kissed them both, and let them sleep. Derek's fate was just sealed forever. She will get rid of him, pushing him away as far as she could, from hers and her children's lives.

After a few days, Ana called a technician to install an intercom in each room, such that she could hear the faintest sound of her babies, everywhere she would be in the house. Shortly after, Derek came with a bunch of papers from the adoption agency, and asked her to sign them. Ana took the papers, tore them to pieces, and threw them into his face, without uttering a single word. His rage was like coming from hell when he shouted:

"You and your bastards will pay for this! I do not want them in my house! I hate them!"

Ana was not moved or scared at all when she said:

"Get out, or I call the police to take and lock you up. You are insane and go somewhere and find help."

Probably he expected to see her frightened or intimidated, because listening to her menacing tone, he gave up his aggressiveness, turned around without replying, and went to the study. After all, he was not that brave when facing such a strong opponent like Ana became. She was watching him like a hawk, being convinced that he will look in finding something to fulfill his wish. Every night before going to bed, she put a mild sedative in his drink to make sure that he will not try to harm the twins while she was asleep. Her life became a nightmare that kept her alert every single minute when Derek was home, but she felt stronger with every decision she had to make.

Ana had one more week left of her maternity leave. She called her mother and asked her to send the nurse that she was supposed to hire. The next day, a short, quite corpulent woman with a round face and a pleasant smile, showed at the door.

"I am Brenda Fox, the nurse "she said.

Ana greeted her with a smile, and invited her in the living room. They sat down, and started a long discussion, Ana telling her about the twins and what exactly she expected from her. She first asked:

"How should I call you, Ms.Fox?"

"Please call me Brenda."

"And you please call me Ana."

When asked about the salary, Brenda mentioned that since there were two babies, the pay will be a little more than her regular compensation for the job, and indicated the sum of money she thought it was acceptable.

"I will pay you double the amount you asked, but you have to assure me that I have nothing to worry, and that you will take care of my babies with your entire capacity of work and skill."

"Ana, you are very generous and I thank you for this. However, you have to know that my work will not be better because of a larger compensation you so kindly offered me. I am a very skilled and dedicated nurse who cared for children all my life. You can be sure that I will never disappoint you, and the babies will have the best care that you can ever expect. You have to trust me."

They both were very pleased with each other. Ana took her upstairs to the nursery; she took the twins one by one, and fell in love with them instantly. Ana gave her all the instructions for the job, and both decided that Brenda should move in the coming Friday, and get accustomed with her new home.

Next day late afternoon, after feeding the babies and making them comfortable in their cribs, Ana went to the kitchen to cook something for dinner. Derek was home in his study. She could clearly hear them prattling through the intercom, when suddenly every sound stopped. Ana took a fireplace poker and rushed upstairs to the nursery. Derek was there standing between the cribs with a pillow in his hands. Ana became livid and rose up the poker.

"What are you doing here? Get out or I will strike you!"

"Nitti, Nitti, you are a very bad girl, poor little mama, and you make very angry the papa, here. I just wanted to make them more comfortable with a pillow under their heads. What else do you think I wanted to do?"

"You are an insane criminal! You wanted to kill them! Get the hell out of here or I will strike you to your death!"

He tried to snatch the poker from her but she pulled back and managed to keep him away from the twins. With hatred in his eyes and a sneer on his face, he left the room. Ana noticed that the intercom was turned off. In those moments of horrible terror, Ana made her final decision: he had to die.

Brenda came as she said, Friday morning, bringing her belongings and a lot of medical stuff that she always carried when she was on the job. Ana helped her to arrange everything in the right place, to make her comfortable and feel that she was welcomed with warmth in her new surrounding that became her home. The next Brenda did, was to change into her uniform, not forgetting the white cap on her head. Ana noticed her quick movements with great assurance in everything she did. In addition, Brenda was like a live stopwatch, because her entire schedule was counted by the minute, not being late with anything on her busy agenda. Ana was amazed by her attitude and her exceptional skill. Taking a neutral tone and like a superficial information,

Ana told her not to let Derek to come close to the babies, because she said, "he cannot handle them, and besides, he has a heart condition and has to avoid any excitement."

The time to go back to work was already there, and next Monday, Ana returned to her lab. On the way, she bought a few boxes with chocolate candies to treat her colleagues after such a long absence. She was greeted with warmth and a round of applauses for the birth of her twins, and with best wishes for happiness. Especially, Miss Marple mentioned that Derek must be extremely excited.

"He is indeed" Ana said.

She went to her place, took her project from where it was left, and started working. Killing microbes was her expertise and she was very good at it. She took three different chemicals, mixed them in a small jar, poured a solution over, and mixed them until the final result became clear. She poured the solution into a very small phial, sealed it, and put it in her pocket.

On her way home, Ana had a lot to think about and many problems to solve. Brenda greeted her at the door of the nursery, reassuring her that everything went well and according to the schedule. She kissed her babies with great love after Brenda asked her to wash first her face and hands. Derek was not home, but he came shortly, and she served him dinner, without either of them uttering a word. Before going to bed, he always took a glass of warm milk. Ana agonized over her conscience but had no choice other than to kill him to save her children. The police had not enough evidence to arrest him or to confine him to a psychiatric institution. She poured only three drops of the solution from the phial; he drank his glass of milk and went to bed. She sat next to him and suddenly all his movements stopped. The terrible monster he became was gone forever. His face was pale, his features were calm, and his mouth showed a shade of a smile. Ana took a deep breath, looked at him, and remembered his answer when long ago after watching the video he made for her, she asked:

"Why are giving me suffering instead of joy?"

"They both go together, side by side, and touch the same chord. All depends on the stimulus that is triggered by the mind and is activated first."

Now if she could ask him "why is he giving her joy instead of suffering", the answer would be the same. She did not feel exactly joy, but a big sense of relief that she did not experienced in a very long time. The poison she gave him could not be detected after more than ten minutes from ingestion and she knew beforehand that the diagnostic will be "sudden cardiac arrest". She turned on all the lights, with heavy steps went to the nursery, and knocked at the door. Brenda showed up and Ana told her between many pauses, that Derek was not breathing. Brenda took her medical bag and rushed to the room, touched his pulse, listened with the stethoscope his heart, and told Ana that her husband was dead.

"What am I going to do?" Ana asked while showing a big sorrow.

"I will call the paramedics and talk to them. You do nothing."

The paramedics came in few minutes, Brenda had a short talk with them, and after examining Derek's body, they took him to the ambulance. Ana said that she will follow them with her car. At the hospital, the doctor said that probably he had a heart attack, but the diagnosis of death will be revealed after the autopsy. He looked with compassion at that young woman who seemed to be crushed by the death of her husband.

"This sort of heart condition happens not only to old people, but also can happen especially to men in their thirties to forties, and even younger. Go home now, my dear, and I will call you after the autopsy will be performed."

Ana went home, with her mind full of thoughts that seemed to struggle in a war zone. First thing in the morning she called her mother and told her in few words what happened. Emily was stunned by the news and said that she will come over and stay for a couple of days. The next call Ana did, was to Miss Marple telling her the same news and that she will be unable to come to work that day and maybe for the rest of the week. Miss Marple was overwhelmed with sadness, expressing condolences and making many comments about such a wonderful man like Derek.

After a couple of days, the doctor from the hospital called Ana and told her what she already knew from the beginning. The diagnose for her husband's death was "sudden cardiac arrest", that can happen in people who appear healthy and do not know they have any heart problems. The body was ready to be removed whenever she will arrange the funerals. Ana called Derek's office, and his friends, and also wrote a long letter to his grandmother without giving her detailed explanations. Emily helped with the arrangements, and Derek's body was exposed in a small church at the cemetery. A big crowd showed up to express condolences and their big regrets for losing such a wonderful friend.

Ana approached the casket, looked at Derek's pale features, and put between his crossed hands her gold pendant with the inscribed word "*Forever*". Inside his jacket she put the video with the love for her that he never could share and died for it. She kissed his forehead and stepped away to make room to people staying in line to show their respect. Ana won the race this time, and as usually before, the loser got the kiss.

The following days she felt numb, like her soul was completely frozen. Ana grew up in a peaceful and harmonious environment and was prepared for a smooth life, to raise a family and be surrounded with love. No one ever told her how to fight dangerous people who threaten to inflict pain and harm upon her. The human beings are equipped with a strong kit of survival that overpowers the thinking process and takes lead in making the right decision when choices are overwhelmed with confusions. Her maternal instinct reacted in the only way she could save the lives of her children, when she had to confront the inevitable danger against which she had no other means to fight. The man who was the love of her life was gone forever, but he took the part of her soul that belonged only to him. He left her with a crippled life for the rest of her days.

Ana stayed home until the end of the week, and her mother was there for her as usually, since she was born. Over dinner, the three of them had long talks about decisions and plans Ana had to make for the future. For the time being she only will take a slower pace with her activities, go to work, and care for the twins together with good nurse Brenda. Later, she might think of making changes or leaving everything just the way it is.

The coming Monday, Ana returned to work, and this time she was greeted with condolences and not with a round of applauses. She was glad to concentrate on her research that kept her thoughts away from the emotional state she has been through for already quite a long time.

After two months, it was already late January next year, Ana asked her mother to recommend her a real estate agent who worked with her father, because she decided to sell the house and buy a new place. Emily knew the right person to do the job, and shortly after, a man in his sixties showed at the door. Ana told him what she expected, and also she described in details what she wanted for a new house to buy in the suburbs on the opposite site of the city.

After about two months a middle-aged couple bought the Eden house, all furnished, giving Ana a fabulous price. The agent took her for a ride to see the house he found, hoping that it was exactly what she asked for. Ana was delighted. The house was located in the suburbs, at the end of a beautiful "Not a Through Street" shaped, with lots of flowers and trees on both sides. She inspected every single spot in details and was very pleased. It was a two stories, four-bedroom house, each with its bathroom upstairs, and a large living room, a study, and a dining room next to a big kitchen with all the amenities, downstairs. All rooms had big windows with lots of light coming trough. A deck upstairs on three sides of the house supplemented the beautiful architectural style. Outside in the back was a covered veranda, quite a big courtroom with thick grass, a few trees, and a swimming pool. Ana could not hope for anything better than that.

She had two weeks to move out of the Eden place where happiness and sorrow were in no shortage for her. For the last time, Ana looked at the house and only her painful soul knew to whom she whispered:

"Farewell"

CHAPTER 2

Midday

A NA AND HER family moved to their new house, taking only their belongings, the music collection, some books, and the nursery.

She also took the marble sculpture of "Eden, the terrestrial paradise with many delights, where the Creator placed the first man and the first woman". New and stylish furniture was bought to suit every room and accommodate everybody's needs. The study was large enough to accommodate a standard size piano, since both Ana and Emily were quite well educated in music, and later, maybe the twins will follow them. Brenda was already a dear member of the family by that time when Elise and Andrew were seven months of age and could stand up easily in their playpen. They already showed two teeth growing, made lots of noises and smiled all the time. They could also say a few syllables close to the words "mama" and "brenda". Emily came over to help with the arrangements in the house, and the three of them spent a lot of time until every thing was in the right place and gave them a big satisfaction. Good copies of Renaissance and Impressionism paintings complemented a warm atmosphere in each room. Brenda had her own bedroom next to the nursery, with a door in-between, where she could arrange her belongings the way she liked, and feel more comfortable having her own place. For the time being, she still wanted to sleep in the nursery to be close to the babies. Here and there, Ana placed the pictures of her family, and in the nursery, she put a big framed photo of herself and Derek, looking and smiling at each other. The children had to know their father, too. After a few days, she hired a young housekeeper to come twice a week for cleaning the house and do the laundry.

Late evening after dinner, Ana liked to take a rest on a chaise lounge on the deck outside, looking at people walking their dogs, at young pairs strolling along the street, or at children plying with parents in front of their houses. It was already the month of April, and she did everything in her power to forget Derek's birthday, without succeeding very well. Looking at the stars above she remembered that once, she was a "Greek goddess dressed in a robe made of celestial stars, and raised on pedestal. A handsome Greek warrior protected her with eternal faithfulness from every one daring to take her away from him". Was it yesterday? Or maybe the day before? On the other hand, perhaps it was such a long time ago that she could not remember when it was. Only her soul knew the tears she carried inside and were deeply buried.

Sometimes, Brenda joined her and they had a long chat. Her parents died when she was very young and she grew up in an orphanage and raised by French nuns. They were good at heart and cared a lot for the children trying to replace the parents whom they never knew. She learned from them to be compassionate and give her love to the unfortunate, to the poor, and the lonely. When the time came for her to leave the orphanage, Brenda decided to become a nurse and care for the sick children. In the beginning, she worked as a maid in the hospital, and went to school at night. It was hard but very rewarding for her when she finished school and graduated as a nurse. She was hired on the spot, and ever since, she dedicated her life to the children who needed her care and her love. She never found the time to have a family of her own, and never had someone close with whom to share her life.

"Now," she said, "Emily, and you, and the twins, are my family that I never had, and that I love and treasure with all my heart."

"We all love you dearly, you are Emily's and mine best friend, and you are a second grandmother to Elise and Andrew."

Brenda burst into tears and was overwhelmed with deep emotions, without being able to say something. Ana took her into her arms, trying to comfort her, and showing her the warmth and love she felt for her. Just to cheer her up she asked:

"Do you think it will be nice to have a dog?"

Brenda wiped her tears and smiled:

"Who's going to walk the dog? I do not need this kind of exercise. Maybe later, when the twins will grow a little bit."

They smiled, embraced each other, and went to bed.

Ana went back to work, without having any more worries to torment her mind. Her children were safe, had the best conditions to grow up and there was no one around to threaten their lives. Every evening she talk to them a lot, telling them stories that certainly they could not understand but those were lessons to teach them new words. They both called her already "mama" every time she was around; they were smiling, prattling, and making lot of noise. They also loved both Brenda and Emily, calling them "Bena" and "Mili". Emily came over every weekend to be with her family and especially to play with the twins. When the weather was good, they all went to the park nearby, to enjoy the fresh air and have a pleasant chat, while the twins were walking and stumbling on the grass. When at home, Ana always put short pieces of harmonious music to promote a cultivated education in this regard for the children. They already showed signs of great pleasure when listening to the piano or violin soloists playing their favorite lullabies.

In September, the twins were one year of age, and they received new toys and a cake from which Brenda allowed them only a small bite. The next day, Ana opened a trust fund account, one for each.

Time went by, and Christmas was already there. Ana had three days off and plenty of time to adorn a big tree and cook a lot for the holidays. Only Emily joined Ana, Brenda, and the twins. They all were happy to be together and close to each other, sharing the best holiday season in a long time. Many times Ana and Emily played by turns, Chopin's ballades in front of their favorite audience, Brenda and the twins who gave them a round of big applauses and showing them the great pleasure they all had. Ana noticed that listening to music the twins reacted differently; Elise paid more attention to violin, while Andrew was more attracted to piano. Both Ana and Emily were fluent in French, and so was Brenda who learned it from the nuns in the orphanage where she grew up. Sometimes they spoke in French and had a big laugh when the twins tried to imitate them and picked a few words. Brenda said that it was too early for them to learn the language since they might mix it with English without knowing the difference. For now, she said, they have to understand the meaning of words in English and to put them together in sentences. The twins gave each other the names they could pronounce much easier: Elise called her brother, "Adi", and Andrew called his sister, "Lisi". The grown-ups took the good example and called them the same. In addition, "Bena" and "Mili" became the official names for Brenda and Emily. They called Ana "Mama" from the beginning and so she stayed.

One day, Emily asked her daughter:

"What do you intend to do with your life from now on? Don't you think that it's time for you to start dating?"

"Mom, please don't lecture me", Ana replied, "I'm doing fine with my life, just the way it is. After you tasted natural coffee, you don't drink surrogate. You know very well what I mean and thank you for your concern."

Emily shrugged her shoulders, and never touched that subject again. She knew her daughter better than anyone else did, and she only tried to see her not suffering anymore, in spite the fact that Ana covered her deep feelings even from her mother.

At work, a couple of her colleagues tried to approach her and invited her to dinner. Ana declined their proposition saying that if she is a widow it doesn't mean that she needs someone to fill in the empty chair next to her. Only thinking about somebody coming close to her, it made her shivering.

Time went by, the twins were three years old and Ana thought that they should start preschool, to be with other children around, and learn many things that will help them with a basic education. They will become exposed to numbers, letters, and shapes. Moreover, they will learn how to socialize, share, and contribute to circle time. She summoned the family to confer on the subject and decide what will be the best to do for the twins. Both Mili and Bena agreed that it will be better for them to have an organized program supervised by a teacher, and which will define their education for the skills required in everyday life.

The next day, the entire family went to the preschool, which was only one block far from the house. The young teacher fell in love with the twins at first sight. They loved talking and telling about their toys, tricycles, contradicting each other, and showing a lot that they are not a bit shy. Ana enrolled them in the program, which started one week before, and they had to come next day for the first time. It was a big event for the entire family, and a lot of excitement. The program was four days a week for three hours daily and started at nine o'clock in the morning.

Next day, Bena took them to the class and was allowed to watch from a corner without the children seeing her. It took only a few minutes for the twins to socialize already with the other children. Without any doubt, both loved their new ambiance, which was different from home, and had many novelties that they found for the first time.

On the way back home, Bena wished to have earplugs, so much, they both talked about the exciting activities they experienced, and mostly about the children, they both liked a lot. In the afternoon, they waited at the door with impatience for Ana to come home from work. When she finally came, they jumped into her arms, competing with each other in telling her about everything, sprinkling now and then a little flower, just to enhance their mother's attention. Ana was no less excited than her children and told them that she was very happy for them, but she said, "when you narrate your story of the day, you should stick with reality and not exaggerate it with what did not happened".

After a few days, the teacher said that both Lisi and Adi had a lot more knowledge about what they were supposed to learn in the program, compared to the other children. She suggested that at home, they should be encouraged to learn more stories and she will ask the twins to narrate them in front of the class. Ana and Bena could not be happier and every evening like before, they kept reading to them, by turn, all kind of stories from children books. More than that, they taught them the alphabet and to put letters together to form short words. In a few weeks both Lisi and Adi could read brief sentences and understand their meanings.

After a while, Ana and Brenda decided that it was the right time for the twins to start learning French. First, they learned simple words about objects around, and gradually advanced in their knowledge by approaching subject easily for them to communicate to each other. They became enthusiastic when they managed to understand and translate their thoughts in both languages without any effort. It was like a play for them especially when they talk to each other, from short sentences to more complicated expressions.

The twins learned a lot in those two years that passed, from both, the preschool program and their family. The time came for them to be enrolled in kindergarten, since they were already five years old. The program was four hours every day, four days a week. Lisi and Adi already knew most of the curriculum, but still they enjoyed a lot the teachings, the atmosphere, the outside activities, and especially the children who all were noisy and playful.

After a little while, Brenda told Ana that it was time for the twins to have each a separate room.

"I can't agree more", Ana said, "Let's see what they think".

She called them and they showed little enthusiasm until their mother explained that they could have their own memorabilia, walls covered with favorite posters, and they even can choose the furniture they like. Nothing will change in their schedule of being together all day long, playing, talking, and going to school. The children became suddenly very enthusiastic and approved with applauses their mother's decision to give each some privacy. She even asked their preference in choosing the room they like most. Since the nursery was the biggest, Ana suggested that Lisi should take that one, and Adi should take the one next to the other side of Bena's bedroom. The twins agreed saying that it was the best choice. Ana told them that it was their responsibility to make the bed, keep the room and closets clean, and not forget to say their prayer before going to bed. The entire family went to the furniture store and Ana let the children to choose whatever they liked. In the next days, their rooms were ready for them to move in, and both Lisi and Adi liked a lot their new place. In the first nights of not being together, they woke up and jumped into Bena's bed, saying that they felt lonely and needed company. Since they were babies, they learned not to be scared of anything and if they would be, Bena and their mother were always there to protect them. One day, Ana asked Bena and Emily if in their opinion the children should start a music program by studying to play an instrument. They both agreed, but suggested before anything to ask them first and see what they think.

"Would you like to learn how to play piano or violin?" Ana asked.

"Yes, Mama!" they both answered in the same time, exploding of excitement.

"I would like to learn violin", Lisi said.

"I would like to learn piano", Adi said.

"So be it. Violin and piano for my favorite players", Ana replied, "we'll go together to the music school in the city and see what they can tell us about what we need"

After a couple of days Ana, Bena, and the children went to the music school which was located quite far from home, and this was one thing that neither of them liked. The Director received them with kindness and said that the children were at the right age to start learning to play an instrument. The conditions were for them either to attain the school twice a week for one hour, or one of the teachers for each child to come home and give them the lessons for a higher cost. Ana chose the second alternative and signed the contract. The Director gave her all the information she needed and the instructions to follow before the first lesson. He called the piano and violin teachers to meet their new students and also gave Lisi a small violin and said:

"Don't try it before your teacher will show you how it works. Take a good care of it and after you finish the course, you will bring it back to me."

"Thank you very much Sir, I promise to take good care of it", Lisi said.

After a pleasant conversation, they all agreed to start the lessons next week, twice a week, for one hour. On the way home, they bought a high chair for piano especially designed for children, to make Adi comfortable, and a violin stand for Lisi.

The next week, the music teachers showed up. Both were young and very pleasant.

"I am Olga, the piano teacher, and this is my colleague Sarah, the violin teacher", one of them said.

After exchanging a few words of courtesy, Ana and the children showed them around, and the first lesson started, with only teachers and students, and none of the grown-ups watching. The house was designed to be soundproofed, such that with the doors closed, neither the violin from Lisi's room, nor the piano from the study could be heard. Ana and Bena, both in the kitchen, waited with impatience the outcome of that new experience in which all of them invested a great hope. After one hour, teachers and students came out, all showing satisfaction and even pleasure.

"We have here promising students, with great will to learn", said both Olga and Sarah, by turns.

The children showed a lot of enthusiasm competing with each other in telling Ana and Bena, how much they both liked their teachers and the lesson.

"Adi has to do thoroughly the assignment I gave him, and practice the lesson fifteen minutes daily for the next session", Olga said.

"The same for Lisi, who seems to like the violin from the first start", said Sarah, "I think we will understand very well each other."

They left, and the children jumped up and down, showing a big excitement, telling Ana, and Bena how much they liked Miss Olga and Miss Sarah, and how kind and delightful they both are.

After one year, both Lisi and Adi, could easily read music and play short musical pieces. They loved playing in front of their family and their teachers who gave them big applauses and congratulations. Practicing every day and following with devotion their teachers' instructions, made them feel confident and willing to become better with every lesson. Music became part of their lives and one beautiful way to express their feelings.

One day, Ana was working at her computer in the study, when Bena showed up standing there and waiting for her attention.

"Good or bad?" Ana asked, "And give it to me straight without any details."

"The children would like to learn swimming and we need your consent. First, we wanted to surprise you, but then we thought that we are not supposed to hide anything from you, since hiding is a first step to lying. We know you better than you think."

"Yes, you know me, and I'm glad you do. Show them in, certainly, they must be outside the door."

They both entered displaying a dignified and yet charming attitude.

"You can learn swimming with some conditions which are very strict and require your responsibility, namely, you will do every daily task the same as usually, you will listen to Bena's instructions without trying to do anything on your own, and you will be careful all the time. If you fail one of these, then I will change the tone of my voice and the subject of our discussion will be very unpleasant for you."

Instead of answering, they jumped into her arms, kissed her on both cheeks, and ran outside. They understood very well what their mother said, and they knew that she was not joking. Bena gave her a kiss too, and ran after the children. Ana lost her disposition of working, and thought how marvelous her children were. She looked at the picture on her desk and whispered:

"Wherever you are, if you are somewhere, look at your children and maybe you will change your feelings and choose not to hate them anymore. I swore to myself, not ever to let them hate you, not because you don't deserve it, but only because I don't want them to carry in their souls the worst, the ugliest, and the most destructive feeling one can have."

One day, they asked about their father. This was the question Ana feared the most. She told them that their father died shortly after they were born, because he was very sick. How to explain about death to six years old children, when even grown ups do not understand the mystery of death? They only saw dead flies and Ana tried to explain them through similitude that dead people are like dead flies, which cannot move anymore, are no longer among living people, and their bodies are set in a special place called "cemetery".

"Did he love us?"

"Yes, he did", Ana answered with the first lie she ever said to them.

The twins were already at the age of school and Ana enrolled them in the first grade. Both were enthusiastic about their new teacher, their classmates, and the curriculum, which was more interesting than everything they learned before. The teacher was young and very pleasant, friendly, and showed big patience with children coming from different background and having a dissimilar level on knowledge. She told Ana that Elise and Andrew were above the level of the other children but they seemed to be very interested in new subjects, like problem solving, and science.

After a couple of months, they made many friends, sharing stories about their families, about their kindergarten times, and about their hobbies.

One day, they asked Ana if she had a little time to talk because they had something very important to say. Their mother always encouraged them to speak up everything they had in mind and share with her all their thoughts and feelings.

"Tell me all about", she said.

"It's about Miguel", Adi started, "he lives far from the school, and rides his bicycle everyday back and forth. A few days ago, he went to the store to buy milk, and his bicycle was stolen. Ever since, he had to walk, he came late to class, and he is always tired. His family is very poor and cannot afford to buy him another bicycle. Lisi and I, we thought that since we use our bicycle only for exercise and pleasure, we can share one, and give to Miguel the other one."

Ana almost, burst in to tears. She took them in her arms and only could manage to say:

"I am very proud of you."

She took a long pause to control her emotion, and continued:

"I'll tell you what we are going to do for Miguel. We are going to the shop and buy a bicycle for him, but he must never know who made him this gift, because we are not going to mention it to him or anyone else. You see, my dearest, when you make a gift to someone, don't expect gratitude or any reward in exchange. People have a certain level of pride that has to be respected, and they are very sensitive when it comes to charity. Any gesture of compassion and of good will no matter how small or big, if displayed openly, makes people to feel uncomfortable and we don't have the right to hurt their feelings. I know that you understand very well what I'm talking about. Do you?"

"Yes, Mama", they both answered at the same time.

"Very well, then. I will talk to the Principal, since he has to know everything that is happening in the school, and after that, we are going to buy the bicycle for Miguel.

She went to school and told the Principal the whole story. He said:

"Your children are not only outstanding students, but also remarkable human beings even if they are so young. Grown up people could take example from them."

Ana could not be more pleased. She asked him what would be the right choice for the bicycle to be delivered, namely, to the school or directly to the family. The Principal said that to the family would be better, since he did not want children and teachers to know about. He gave her the address, and fell into deep thoughts after she left.

In the same day, Ana and the twins went to the shop to make the buy, not before asking them how tall was Miguel. They said he was shorter then them, and they picked the right size and color. Ana specified all the conditions for delivery, mentioning that no name of the sender should be indicated on the package.

The next afternoon, both Lisi and Adi waited with great joy for their mother to come home and tell her about Miguel, how happy he was.

"He kept repeating over and over again that someone unknown sent him a bicycle as a gift, and his mother wanted to thank from the bottom of her heart to that person who showed so much compassion for their family", Lisi said.

"But of course, nobody knew", Adi said "and everybody wished him well and advised him to take better care of his bicycle."

"This makes you feel good? Much better than Miguel had come to you and showed his gratitude?" Ana asked.

"Oh, yes, much better. I think we both feel a lot of joy", Lisi said, and she added, "Miguel mentioned that his mother named God as helping them. Who is God?"

"Same as we call 'Creator' and you recognize this name better, since you were three years old and said your first prayer. I taught you then to express in your own words before going to sleep, your thoughts and your feelings about what you did that day, if you were good or bad, not trying to hide anything and not lying. Remember? I told you that the Creator made us all and He only asks from us to tell the truth always to ourselves and to the other people. I also told you that your prayer is a very private conversation between you and your Creator, and is not supposed to be commented by anyone, not even by your mother. Since you are older now, I shall tell you, that people are created to make their own choices before taking the right decision, and not ask the Creator for helping them until they use every bit of their resources to solve no matter how difficult situation they encounter. Now, you know a little more about who God or the Creator is, and I am always here for you to answer any question you have, if I can".

"This was so beautiful!" Adi exclaimed.

"I would like to know more about the Creator", Lisi said.

"I tell you what. We all go this evening late, outside on the deck and we can talk a little bit more about Creation. What do you say?"

"Sounds great!" they both answered.

That evening they went on the deck, Ana took them on her sides, and Bena joined them. The sky was clear and it was a quiet night with trillions of stars above, like waiting to tell their story. Ana started:

"You learned in school about the sun, moon, and the stars. Let us go a little farther. Look up at the sky, and you can see so many stars that no one can count them. Some are blinking and those are called 'stars', and they are like our sun, which gives light and makes us feel warm. Others, are not blinking, those are 'planets' or similar bodies and they are like our earth, but you can see them shining because they receive light from the stars around. Everything you see is called the 'Universe' and it was created much before people were born on Earth. Every single star and planet in the universe has a precise spot that was designed by the Creator, and is subjected to the control of very strict laws, such that they have to follow a defined path of their movements, and are not allowed to spread apart. You must know that everything was created for a reason, and has a special meaning to be. The Earth was chosen by the Creator to be the place where people are born, can grow up, work, have families, and make choices to build their lives. You cannot see the Creator like a person, but His divine presence is in everything He created. Everything in the universe and in our natural habitat, represents His work that started in the long past of time that cannot be known. If He could be seen, then people would be in line to ask for help, for everything they need or want to have, and they would become like vegetables without means to grow by using their minds. People give rewards, impose punishments, and make their own laws to be obeyed by everybody in an organized society. The Creator interferes in our lives only after we used all our resources to solve the difficulties we encounter, and only then, He shows us the right path to follow. He gives no rewards for good deeds we accomplish, and He does not punish us for what we do bad. And you know why? Because in His greatest love for people, He let us judge ourselves for everything we do, we feel, and intend to work for our future. We must say that we love our Creator by loving and respecting His magnificent work. My cherished ones, this concludes our story for tonight. Think about it, and you will find more in books and on the computer if you want to expand your knowledge."

The children were excited. They both tried to speak in the same time. Lisi came first:

"This was a wonderful story, Mama. I wished you never stopped talking. You know so much about everything."

"Is there anything that you don't know?" Adi asked.

"I know very little from the entire knowledge that exists. However, if I want to know something that I need, I always can read books, search on the computer, or learn from people. I advise you to do the same, you will have big satisfactions, and you will never cease looking for what makes knowledge a source in finding the truth."

"Ana, I join Lisi in saying that I wished you never stopped talking." Bena said, "You should be a teacher. Now, children let's give her a big kiss and go to bed."

They all kissed her and called the night off. The children will have something marvelous to talk to each other for a long time.

After few days, Ana came home and saw them all three waiting for her on the couch in the living room. Adi had some bandages on his arms and legs, and band-aides on his face. Her first impulse was to scream like hell, but she managed to control her feelings and asked Bena:

"Does he need a doctor?"

"No. I checked him very thoroughly, and he has some bruises and scratches. Nothing serious and nothing to worry about."

Ana took her place in the armchair and said:

"Lisi talk to me."

"You see…Anthony picked on Jesse…for no reason…saying that his father was a drunkard… and Jesse is very small…and the shortest in class… and he started yelling at Anthony and Anthony… who is tall like Adi… but much larger… started punching him … and his nose… started bleeding… and then Adi jumped between them…and tried to pull them apart… and then

Anthony started to punch Adi… and then Adi punched him back… and then they both fell down… and then they started wrestling… and then the Principal came over… and pulled them apart… and then the Principal asked what happened… and then Adi said that it was a minor… dispute and then…the Principal said that if… something like that …will ever happen again… they both… will be suspended for one week… and then he asked them to shake hands…and that was all what happened."

Ana asked her to come over, made her sit on her lap, and said:

"Let us both analyze the situation and see who was wrong and who was right. First, Anthony did not have right to talk about Jesse's father and he had no right to hurt him. Therefore, Anthony was wrong. Jesse was brave and wanted to protect his father's reputation even if he had to face someone stronger than he was. Therefore, Jesse was right. Adi tried to pull them apart and solve the conflict peacefully, but without success, since Anthony started to punch him. Adi showed what everyone must do, namely, that he had to defend someone who cannot defend himself. On all counts, Anthony was wrong, Jesse was right, and Adi was right."

Ana reserved for herself her conclusion about the Principal who was wrong since he did not bother to analyze the situation in details and jumped directly to his final decision, and that was to punish them both next time something similar will happen. She kept Lisi in her arms and made her to pay attention to what she was about to tell her:

"I appreciate very much the explaining of the entire situation. However, when you narrate a story, try to use a fluent language and not stumble into your own words. I know that you were very much involved into your brother's condition, but please keep under control your emotions and think straight without being scared."

She asked Adi to come close, and embraced him with all her warmth and love:

"I am very proud of you. The way you judged the situation was outstanding, in my opinion. I know that you have a good feeling about yourself, and a great trust in your capability of making the right decisions. Just be careful and make sure that you don't get hurt."

In the coming weekend, Emily came, and they all went to the park to enjoy a beautiful sunny day. The children played with the ball, running and making new friends about their age. Summer vacation was almost there, and they all had to make a plan to spend it together and make the best of it. Ana suggested a trip to the ocean, and have a good time in a first class hotel, swimming, strolling on the beach, and enjoying the fresh air.

"I think that two weeks will be enough and after that we'll do something else", Ana said.

"Are we going to drive?" asked Bena.

"Oh, no. There are too many hours of driving and the children will be tired. We are going by plane, and this will be less than two hours."

"Then you and the children go. Emily and I, we both are scared of flying, and we'll stay home."

"We are not going without you two. We all stay home then, and we'll make some other plans. There are plenty of things we can do and enjoy together a good time."

Before going home, the children asked their mother to tell them the story of the ants, because she promised so. Ana told them, this time in French, the story of the ants, while they all watched the minuscule insects running back and forth on the ground. She told them first that those little creatures live in a colony and a precise law of the nature guides their life, which is part of the Creation. The colony has a queen, which takes care of the heredity, then there are the soldiers, who protect the queen and the colony, and then there are the workers, which look for food and store it in special chambers, making sure that every member will have enough to eat during the wintertime. She told them that an ant can lift twenty times its own body weight. Finally, there are the sitters who take care of the babies, just as people do. Ants do not have ears. They "hear" by feeling vibrations in the ground through their feet. Like most insects, ants have compound eyes made from numerous tiny lenses attached together. Overall, the ants are organized in a society with a very strong structure that made them one of the best surviving species over hundreds of million of years.

"Think about this story, and if you want to know more, read books and search on the computer."

Ana thought that what she told them would be enough for the level of their understanding and knowledge. The children were excited like every time their mother told them stories. They had a new interesting subject to talk about for a while.

One day, Ana asked Bena:

"By the way, how are the swimming lessons going?"

"Why don't you come and watch? I'll tell you why, because you never have time for that. You bring work at home, lock yourself in the study, and keep your nose in the computer and in your papers until night, and then you are exhausted and go to bed. That's why!"

When did she hear similar words? Yes, she remembers, it was a very long time ago.

"What do you want me to do? The project I'm working on requires a lot of research which is essential for the results, and there is not enough time to do it in the lab."

"Since you asked me, I suggest to do whatever you can in your lab, and not to bring work at home. Then, you will know more about your children."

Bena was right, Ana thought. Her children, their growth, and their development were more important than anything else was.

The coming Saturday morning, she watched them swimming and was amazed. They both could go all the way from one side to the other of the pool with ease and without pause. She joined them and all three had the most wonderful time, planning to do it again.

Summer vacation was already there. Both Lisi and Adi graduated from first grade with straight "A", and were ready to enjoy a two months vacation until they will start school in fall. Ana had also four weeks to spend with her family. There were many things to do and enjoy, pleasing everyone and all together. She asked the children first if they had a special request for summer activities. They both wanted a little more time outside, and have some physical exercise. Ana took them to a gym club to watch a class of children about their age, and if they like the place and what they do, she will enroll them in the program, which was one hour a day, three times a week. Both were very pleased, and Ana talked to the trainer to find out about the program. They will have gymnastics, ball games, running, and initiation into karate.

After a few sessions, the children were so captivated by the program that they wanted to continue it even during the school time. Ana said that first, they have to know the requirements of the second year of school, and after, they will decide if they could continue with the program. She was no less happy than her children were.

Their music advancement showed a lot of progress with every passing day. The practice was followed according to a strict schedule increasingly complex with lots of repetition and new pieces to learn.

In that summer, Ana introduced them to Opera and as a first experience for them, she chose Puccini's "La Bohème". She bought an entire loge close to the stage for the whole family, but before, she told the children to pay attention more to the music than to the subject, since almost all opera lyrics are dramatic and might feel them uncomfortable. She told them the subject so that they could follow the story much easier. The children followed the entire spectacle without moving.

After the last applauses, Lisi said:

"The music is superb, but I wished to understand the words. I would like very much to learn Italian since I intend to go often to the Opera House when I'll grow up."

Adi could not agree more. He too liked the music a lot but wished to understand the lyrics also.

"Can we learn Italian, Mama?" he asked.

"Well, my dearest ones, I only can tell you that I could not be of any help in this subject, since I don't know the language and neither Bena nor Mili do. But, I suggest checking your schedule thoroughly, and if you have time to spare, we can buy the package for you to watch, and this could be of much help, if you agree. Your schedule should include every single task you have to perform daily, comprising books reading. Don't let your excitement make you overlook the basic tasks you have to carry out. Consult each other and let me know your decision."

Both children applauded with great enthusiasm, and in the same day, they decided that there was enough time to spare for learning the new language. They got the package of Italian, and both Ana and Bena were very curious to see how they would manage to do this one too.

The next Saturday they all went to the Concert Hall to attend Bruch's Violin Concerto nr.1 played by a Chinese soloist. It was a marvelous spectacle indeed, and especially Lisi was like charmed. The children were quite well accustomed with concert spectacles since they watched at home lots of videos, but never saw one live on stage. The next concert was especially chosen for Adi, and that one was Liszt's Piano Concerto nr.1, played by an American young girl soloist who recently graduated from the Conservatory. It was indeed a real treat for the children who exploded with shouts and applauses.

In that summer, they went four times to the Opera House, and three times to the Concert Hall.

In fall, the children started the second grade. The curriculum was more extensive with new science concepts to more complex math operations, and reading challenges that were more comprehensive.

One day, a friend from college, Mark by his name, called Ana and invited her to diner, just to talk about old good times. She declined his invitation but he kept calling her again every day. Adi said to her:

"Why don't you go with him and enjoy yourself a little bit? Poor guy calls you every day, and we are not against you having dinner with him."

"When I'll ask your permission, then you'll give it to me. Until then, abstain yourself from giving me advice."

After a few more calls, Ana accepted the invitation and Mark showed at the door with a bouquet of flowers.

They went to dinner and he did all the talking, mostly about his recent divorce and about his wife, while Ana kept silence most of the time. He asked her to meet again and Ana said that she was not interested in a relationship, and it was better not to see each other again. Back home, the children were very curious to know how the date evolved.

"I did not have such a boring time in my life", she said, "and this concludes any further explanations, since there is nothing for me to add."

"This is because you expect people to be smart like you, and if they are not, you don't like them", Lisi said.

"Just to give you satisfaction, I agree with you.

Try to know yourself and measure your potential with fairness. Always remember that there is unfailingly someone out there above you and someone below you. If you know how to set your standards at the right level, you will always know how to evaluate your friends and how to avoid unfriendly people. Now please change the subject or go to whatever you have to do."

Indeed, there was no one out there to please her or making her to have at least some friendly feelings. Everything in her soul regarding a relationship, was cold dead.

One day when Ana was working in the study both Adi and Lisi jumped into her arms and asked:

"What means the name 'Eden' on that sculpture? We asked Mili and Bena and they don't know. They said to ask you."

"According to a very old legend Eden was 'the terrestrial paradise with many delights, where the Creator placed the first man and the first woman' to have a family and raise their children. It is said that it was the beginning of the humankind."

"Who gave the sculpture to you?"

"I bought it from the Art Gallery, many years ago, and I thought that is a symbol of a happy place."

"It shows a real place that can be seen?"

"Somewhere it could be, but it is just a legend."

Assumably they were satisfied and left, leaving Ana with a shivering soul and being grateful that no more questions followed.

Time went by, two more years passed, the children grew just like their mother wanted them to be, and every one in the family was happy to take care of each other like always. Their Italian learning seemed to go smoothly since they were able to have short conversations with each other and liked a lot the language. Amazingly enough, they learned alone, without any help. Ana bought them story books in Italian to enhance their learning, and their own library with all the books they had, was remarkably big. They were already ten years old when Ana received a long letter from Oma, asking her for a visit together with the children. She replied that in summer they might come over to see her. Ana talked to the children and they both were enthusiastic to make a trip overseas and see their great grandmother and especially the place where their father was born and grew up.

In summer vacation, Ana booked a trip to Heidelberg on a night flight. The children wanted Mili and Bena to join them but their mother said that they were not invited, so they had to stay home. On the plane, both Lisi and Adi were very comfortable, not showing a bit of scare. They arrived early in the morning, and since nobody was there to meet them, they took a cab and went to the address. Both Oma and Gretchen, the housekeeper, greeted them at the door, embracing them and inviting them inside. The children were impressed by the grandiosity of that house, with all those carved oak doors with beveled glass, the staircase, the crystal chandelier, and everything around that they never saw before.

Charlotte looked at both children and said:

"You are so beautiful and tall for your age. Call me Grand Oma since I am your great grandmother. I hope you will like spending a few days with me, and we can talk about your school, your hobbies, and about the family. Gretchen will give you now a tour of the house, and show you to your rooms, while your mother and I, we'll have a little chat."

She asked Ana about her life as a widow, and how she managed to raise the twins without their father. Ana told her that she did the best she could and asked the old woman not to mention the childhood of their father. Oma promised not to say them anything that might raise questions for which there were not proper answers.

The children looked around and asked for more pictures of their father and grandparents, noticing the unusual beauty of their grandmother Louise. After an entire day of talking and telling Oma everything she wanted to know about their lives, they all went to bed. Ana and Lisi, both shared a room with a huge bed, while Adi was escorted by Gretchen to a room next to them. Lisi was too tired to express her impressions about all the excitement of that day and postponed the talking for later. When both were almost asleep, Adi showed at the door, telling Ana that he could not sleep in that room and jumped next to his mother.

"Since when are you scared of the dark?" she asked.

"I am not scared of the dark. I am scared of being alone in that room. Nothing is friendly there or in this house. It gives me goose pumps."

"Go to sleep now, and we'll talk about this tomorrow."

She kissed them both, thinking that maybe her son was right.

The next morning Ana asked Gretchen to put a bed in the room because Adi was not familiar with the place and he felt uncomfortable being alone. After breakfast, Oma asked the children to sit on her sides and invited Ana to sit in the armchair when she addressed the twins:

"This house with everything inside will be yours after I die. You will have a nice place to move in or use it like a vacation house every time you travel to Europe. I also opened a trust fund for you, and you can access it when you will be twenty years old. Well? Do you agree with my decision?"

Both Lisi and Adi looked at their mother who answered:

"You are very generous Oma, but maybe it will be better to change your will and leave everything to one of your relatives who needs the house more than Lisi and Adi."

"I have no close relatives, my dear, and the twins are my grandson's children. Everything I have goes to them."

"We all must thank you very much for your notable gift, which is more than impressive" Ana said, and added: "Children, show your gratitude to Grand Oma, for her kindness and for her love."

They both kissed her, saying one after the other, that they never expected such a great gift and they both will think about her and how generous she is.

After that conversation they all felt like going out and Ana gave them a tour of the neighborhood and maybe the next days she will show them the interesting places of Heidelberg. They showed little enthusiasm and she thought that it was maybe too much for them to absorb everything that was different from what they knew. Memories of the past brought only sadness in her soul and she would have liked not to be there. They went to the park and sat on a bench, and Adi said:

"I don't want that house. Lisi can have it all if she wants it. It gives me a bad feeling which scares me."

"I don't want it either," Lisi said." Everybody who lived in that house died. It is like a ghost house, and gives me a creepy feeling. I want to go home to Bena and Mili and our house, and our neighborhood, and our friends, and our school. Let's go home, Mama."

"Yes, let's go home, Mama" Adi said, "Grand Oma is very nice but I want to go home."

Ana had a big sigh. She felt no better than her children.

"Let's make the best of this situation the way we can", she said, "we are her guests and her family. We have to stay for the time we booked our trip. Will you try and bear with me?"

They both agreed that a few more days would not be so hard to spend there.

The following days were more pleasant since Ana showed them the historic monuments and sites in the Old Town. They went to the Old Bridge with the gate and two towers and most of all, Ana wanted them to visit the Heidelberg University and its Library. At least these much they both liked a lot.

Time for returning home was there. All three embraced Grand Oma and Gretchen, thanking them for their great hospitality, and for being such good hosts to them. The next day both Mili and Bena greeted them at the airport. The children jumped into their arms, holding them tightly as if they wanted to make sure that they both were for real and not a dream.

"What is going on with you?" asked both Mili and Bena.

"They missed you very much", Ana said. "Let's go home."

They arrived home and the children rushed to the door, went inside and started jumping up and down, shouting like savages. They ran upstairs, opened all doors, as if making sure that nothing changed during their trip. Bena said that lunch was ready, and all took their places around the table.

"How was your vacation over there?" Mili asked, "somebody starts talking."

"Tell them", Ana said.

Both Lisi and Adi told them everything not missing any detail. They also mentioned that nothing there pleased them and they were eager to come home.

"Grand Oma said that she will leave us the house with everything inside, but we don't want that house. It's creepy", Adi said.

There were no comments, and no more explanations to ask. Every one was happy to be together and close to each other. After one week, the children started the school; they were already in fifth grade, which was the last year of elementary school, and they had many new things to learn. They also had to continue with music lessons, gym sessions, and books reading. One day, Lisi asked Emily:

"Why she never talks about our father? We know very little about him."

"Because it's very painful for her to talk about him. He was the love of her life, they were young when they got married and she lost him shortly after you were born. They adored each other and had big plans for a wonderful future that never was fulfilled. Your father was highly educated, very knowledgeable, and a very skilled architect. They were made for each other. Besides, he was very handsome, and you both have some of his features. I have never seen two people loving each other like they were."

"Too bad that he died and we were not able to know him", said Adi.

"Yes, too bad" Emily completed the explanation, without saying anything else that was in her mind.

If the children were satisfied with what she told them, no one knew, but they never brought up that subject again.

Ana got a promotion at work, with increase in her salary, which made her saving account to become more substantial. She made some good investments in real estate and doubled her money in a short time. Her children were well insured, the house was already paid, and she intended in the far future to buy a house for one of the children, such that each one will own a good place to live with the new family they will start.

For the time being, she gave up bringing her work at home, and she paid more attention to their activities. One day she was in the study while the children practiced their music lessons. Suddenly she almost stopped breathing. Lisi was playing Rimsky Korsakov's the violin solo from *Scheherazade*. Ana's soul was like bleeding. He chose for her that music when the first time she asked him to play something for her. He played it again in the video he made for her and she was crying for so much love he showed her. She cried now without trying to wipe her tears. Indeed, he will never let her go, as he always said. Before her children, she smiled all the time, using a soft and warm voice, while her soul was screaming of the big pain carried deep inside and that she tried so hard to hide.

Adi asked her one day:

"How old are you?"

"This is not a nice question to ask a lady."

"You are not a lady. You are our mother."

"Which makes me what?"

"This makes you the most loved being in the whole world."

"Well, then I have to tell you, but don't be disappointed. I am thirty-seven years old. Why are you asking?"

"Because you have already white hair and at your age you are not supposed to have white hair, this is what Bena said and she also said to ask you. Why do you have white hair?"

"Probably because my biological organism is set to work like that. Everyone is different even if people's bodies are similar. Are you satisfied?"

"For now. When I'll grow up I'll ask you again and then maybe you will have another answer, more precise."

"I think that you are very smart for your age. Mind your own business, and don't be concerned about my white hair."

He left without telling her that both he and Lisi saw her too many times plunged into deep thoughts and trying to hide a shade of sadness that none of them could explain, but they both learned from Bena that sadness makes people to have white hair.

The music teachers told Ana that the Director would like very much to audit the children since they told him what a big progress they both made in the past year. He is expecting to see them Saturday morning at ten, if this is acceptable for Ana. She agreed and the entire family went to the music school as decided. The Director greeted them, took a seat in the auditorium, and Ana, Mili and Bena took their seats behind him. The children were on the stage waiting for him to start the audition.

"Elise, first" he said. "What are you going to play for us?"

"Rimsky Korsakov-*Capriccio Espagnol.*"

Lisi arranged her notes on the stand and started playing. Adi was next to her, turning the pages. The expression on her face stirred long time passed memories that were deeply buried into Ana's soul.

Lisi finished the piece and took a bow before the audience.

"Thank you Elise," the Director said, "now is your turn Andrew. What are you going to play?"

"Chopin - *Nocturne Op9 no1 in B flat Minor.*"

Adi took the seat at the piano and started playing while Lisi turned the pages. Ana had no idea that her son could play such a masterpiece. After he finished, he took a bow, and both Lisi and him waited for the verdict.

The Director went to the stage, shook hands with them, and said:

"Outstanding, both of you. I must say that I never expected such a splendid performance. Congratulations to you both, and I express all my best wishes for your further accomplishments."

He turned to Ana and said:

"They have a great aptitude. Have you thought to pursue a musical career for them?"

"It is for them to decide, and it is too early I think. Whatever they will like to do later, they will have my entire support. For the time being, music is a big pleasure for them and in my opinion they should continue studying with their teachers, who gave them such a wonderful musical education."

"I shall keep in mind and wait for them to grow. I will be here for them. Now, I would like them to play for a big audience at the twenty-fifth anniversary of the school, and this will be two weeks from now. It will be a good exposure for them and a great honor for the school. Would this be acceptable for you?"

"The honor is for me, and I must thank you for the confidence you have in my children, but you have to ask them first."

Both Lisi and Adi showed a big interest and promised to play with their entire competency in front of the audience.

For the next two weeks, they practiced every day, and they will play the same solo pieces that were appreciated by the Director at the audition. Lisi returned the small violin to the school last year and she played already on a three quarter size. Beside their solo performance, they were assigned to accompany each other and play one piece together.

Next Saturday, the children dressed up like for a gala, and the entire family went to the music school for the big event.

"Are you nervous?" Ana asked.

"Not a bit", they both answered in the same time.

They arrived at the school a little earlier, the children went back stage, and the family took seats in the middle of the third row. Shortly after, the auditorium was full packed, and the Director gave a speech about the significance of that event, mentioning that the most gifted students will perform in front of the audience, starting with the youngest ones. After three children played their parts, and received big applauses, Lisi and Adi were presented, and started their repertoire. Each one, received ovations from the audience, which showed a big enthusiasm for those two children only ten years old. The biggest success was when Lisi and Adi played together Dvorak- *Romance for piano and violin.* They both looked so absorbed in the music, that probably none of them paid any attention to the public. Ana had in her mind the same thought as she had long time ago: "Wherever you are, if you are somewhere, look at your children and maybe you will change your feelings and choose not to hate them anymore."

After they finished, the spectators exploded in a standing ovation and applauses. They took each other's hand and bowed with grace in front the audience. They were called three times on the stage, and played for encore, Beethoven- *Für Elise- Piano and Violin duet.*

All three, Mili, Bena and Ana were overwhelmed with emotions, not being able to make any comments. On the way back home, the children competed with each other in expressing their reactions and feelings. Ana made no effort to control her joy and happiness when she said:

"I have not enough words to tell you how proud I am. You were both outstanding in your performances. I must say that you both amazed me. I could listen over and over to your repertoire, without having enough of it."

They both jumped into her arms, kissing her with all their love. Mili and Bena, still under deep emotions, said that they join Ana in her appreciation for the way they both performed, and were very happy for their success.

Later that year, Ana received a letter from Gretchen, saying that Grand Oma died and maybe she should come for the funerals.

"We are not going", both Lisi and Adi said.

"Nobody invited you. I have to go."

"Now you can sell the house and make some money," Adi suggested.

"I cannot sell it because you two are the owners and it will be your decision what to do with it, when you will be twenty years old."

The next evening, Ana flew to Heidelberg, took a cab to the house, and Gretchen met her at the door. The following day, she joined quite a big crowd who knew well the family and went to the funerals. On the way back Gretchen asked her intentions about the house; Ana told her that for the time being nothing will change and she could live there for as long as she wanted. Ana was quite sure that Gretchen will sell lots of things, but it was not her concern and she could not care less. She was eager to go home, and thought that her children were right when they said that everybody who lived there, died. Indeed, that house was creepy.

The children were not even curious about the trip. They were happy to see her safe and close to them. Both Lisi and Adi told her with big excitement that they received already the green belt for their karate skill, meaning that they will now be required to acquire in-depth expertise of the practiced karate moves.

"I am really pleased with your progress in this one too. Make sure not to practice your expertise at school and not pick a fight with your classmates. I'll be glad to watch you one of these days."

She asked Bena to accompany her to see the children at the gym, but Bena said that she watches them twice a week when she drives them to the training program. For a change, she said, it was Ana's turn to go and watch her children punching each other. Ana was enthusiastic by the way both mastered the karate skill. The trainer praised both Lisi and Adi for the progress they show with every session, and told Ana that it will be very good for them to come three or four times weekly instead of twice. This was one proposition that Ana declined quickly, saying that their schedule was very tied and they will not be able to do more than that.

Three more years passed by. Lisi and Adi were almost fourteen years old, they were tall, quite athletic, and beautiful in mind and body. They were at the age of puberty or so, and Ana called Bena to help in that delicate subject.

"Nothing to worry about. I told them everything they are supposed to know" Bena said, "they are well prepared and understood everything I taught them. I was sure that you would not be able to be mother and father this time, as you usually are. I will also teach Adi how to shave when time will come. He already shows a little shade of moustache and checks it in the mirror all the time."

"You are a blessing, Bena."

"I know. And you all are my family that I love and cherish."

After few days, Ana summoned the family for an important meeting. They all were curious to find out what was that all about.

"This coming summer, the children will have two months vacation and I have my four regular weeks to which I shall add two more weeks of leave without pay. I thought that we all should go to Italy, and visit Rome, Florence, Milan, and Venice. What do you think?"

The children jumped with joy and big excitement. Mili and Bena showed no enthusiasm at all.

"I cannot go", Mili said "First, because I don't have more than three weeks vacation, second, that I cannot leave my patients who need me, and third, because I am scared of flying."

Ana and the children were disappointed. It was Bena's turn to answer:

"I am scared to fly, and this makes me say that I have not a bit of enthusiasm. On the other hand, I cannot stay home alone, without you for such a long time. Therefore, I will try to overcome my fear of flying and I will go with you."

She received a round of applauses and a big kiss from everybody. Ana said that she will book the trip and include the best hotels reservations, hoping that the four of them will have a wonderful time. She also suggested especially to the children to read some art books and learn mostly about the Renaissance period, such that they will be prepared to acquire new knowledge in that trip.

"You can find many art books in the study, and you better start reading", she said.

Summer time was already there, and they were ready for the trip. Ana told them to pack only one suitcase for each, and if they will need something there, they will buy. She also gave to every one quite a bit of money, saying that was all for the entire trip but they were free to buy whatever they will like. They boarded a night flight and arrived to Rome early in the morning.

"It wasn't that bad as I thought" Bena said, "I even got a good night sleep."

"Glad to hear that" Ana said, "now let's take a cab and go to the hotel. People here speak well English, but I want you Lisi and Adi, to use your Italian everywhere like a good practice, and besides we will receive a better service. For a start, Adi since you are the man in the family, tell the driver the address of our hotel."

On the road, both spoke Italian with the driver, and who knows what story they told him, because he laughed and was very pleased.

The hotel was located few steps from Villa Borghese, the second largest landscape garden in the naturalistic English manner in Rome.

After registering, the guest Assistant showed Ana a lot of courtesy, since they checked in a luxurious suite and certainly, he knew where to smell money. A bellboy took their luggage and escorted them to the suite. It was luxurious indeed, and from the balcony there was a display of the entire city.

"This is something like in a wonderful dream", Bena and both children said by turn.

After checking the place and making sure that each one was comfortable with the accommodation, they went downstairs to have a hearty breakfast.

The restaurant was above expectations and both Lisi and Adi, ordered for everybody after asking what they liked.

When Ana was about their age, her parents took her to Italy, they visited Rome and Florence, but on a much lower budget. It was a long time ago and she kept dear memories of that vacation.

After savoring those dishes with great pleasure, they went to their suite, started unpacking and making plans for the day.

"Are we going to rent a car?" Adi asked.

"We don't need a car. Rome is a small city, we can walk easily from one side to the other, and besides, it has a very good public transportation. Let's see where we start our first day in this friendly city. Here is a good brochure, and I suggest first to get accustomed with the neighborhood. Take your cameras and make pictures as many as you want, but pay attention to signs where are prohibited. We don't need any trouble with the authorities."

They walked to the Borghese garden, which was nearby, then went to the Spanish Steps with the church Trinità dei Monti on top and to Trevi Fontana. Tourists like them were everywhere on the streets looking for attractions and places to visit. Ana told them:

"Italian people like to take a long rest after lunch and most of the shopping places are closed until four or five in the afternoon. We can go back to the hotel, or we can go farther and look around. If you are hungry, we can eat at a 'trattoria' and then go to visit the roman forum."

They did just like that. The knowledge about the sites they visited was shared between them with many comments especially from the children. It was evening already when they returned to the hotel. Ana told them that next day they will go to the Vatican and visit the St. Peter's Basilica and the Sistine Chapel. Early morning they took the bus and went to the Vatican. They all agreed that the Basilica was rather a museum than a place of worship. It was impressively big and the contribution of Michelangelo to the architecture and to the artistic exhibits was awesome. Especially The Pietà made a profound effect on the children's feelings. The many pictures they saw in books were not even close to the real masterpiece.

They went to the Sistine Chapel and were even more amazed by the beauty of the paintings and the subjects depicted on the ceiling and walls. The children knew the whole story of the chapel and about the relationship between Michelangelo and the Pope Julius II.

"To visit the Vatican Museum", Ana said, "we'll need more than one day and I suggest that we shall do this tomorrow. Now, maybe you will like to go shopping and visit the many boutiques, which offer plenty of souvenirs."

They went shopping and bought whatever they liked, until almost evening when returning to the hotel they had a big dinner and went to bed. The next day was full of excitement when visiting the Vatican museum, which probably required a long period to be seen in details. It was already evening when they entered a restaurant on the Tiber River bank where an orchestra played beautiful dance music. Everybody was hungry, but the children were very tempted by the music and joined other dancers on the floor.

"When did you learn how to dance?" Ana asked.

"Bena taught us" Lisi answered, "she learned from the nuns."

Ana had a sigh before saying:

"Dear, good friend Bena, is always there to my rescue."

Adi escorted his sister to the table, and came before his mother, bowed with courtesy, and said:

"May I have the pleasure of this dance, Madame?"

He was about her height and proved to be a wonderful dancer. Ana was no second fiddle to her son either. After finishing, Adi kissed her hand and escorted her to the table, inviting this time Bena with the same courtesy he showed for Ana.

After a pause, he asked Lisi for a dance.

"How come you don't bow and show me no courtesy?" she asked.

"Don't push my manners too far. Let's go dancing."

Ana and Bena looked at them with nostalgia thinking and talking about the many years passed since they were just babies.

In the following days, they visited most of the museums mentioned in the brochures, and many churches with deep roots in the history of the past. They all concluded that all churches were more like museums displaying splendors of painting and sculpture, but hardly could be considered places of worship.

After the many points of attraction they covered every day, it was time to leave Rome and take the next step to Florence, which is renowned for its high concentration of Renaissance art and architecture. They took the train in the morning and arrived in Florence after one hour and a half. The hotel was similar to the one in Rome but with richer wall and ceiling paintings and had a grand view over the Botanical Gardens. Ana told them:

"Florence is smaller than Rome, and we will be able to walk to all of the sites. Its history does trace back to the Romans and it earned its place as the center of the Renaissance."

In that first day a stroll on the neighboring streets was the best choice, just to get a sense of the scale of the city and to plan a schedule for the next day. They walked to the "Piazza della Signoria", a beautiful square where tourists had a relaxing time over a coffee or snack served at tables outside the restaurants. From there they went to the Ponte Vecchio Bridge and visited the tiny shops, interrupted by two wide terraces, which opened out on to an incredible view of the river Arno.

Back at the hotel, they changed many impressions about that day, over a savory dinner in the restaurant. Next morning they first visited the "Gallery of the Academy" which certainly is the most famous for its sculptures by Michelangelo. There, his Prisoners (or Slaves), his St. Matthew and, above all, the outstanding statue of David displayed his magnificent work.

In that first week, they visited "Palazzo Vecchio" famous for its beautiful frescoes, sculptures, and painted ceilings, "Palazzo Pitti" housing several museums, and "Santa Maria del Fiore", the domed cathedral that is often called the "Duomo". Known today as the world's largest masonry dome, this majestic cathedral features 600 years worth of stunning architecture and art works.

"It is very hard to absorb so much information in such a short time," Lisi said.

"This trip is more like an initiation into the arts and Art History. You always have plenty of books to enhance your knowledge", Ana replied.

"I like very much the architecture of this city, and I think that I will study it later and become an architect," Adi said.

"It runs in the family on your paternal side", Ana mentioned.

"I don't care about that. Don't ask me to pay merit to people who never did anything for me and I never knew. In addition, you know what? I will be much better than them, because I will study also Art History."

His remark impressed Ana, but she said nothing.

In the second week, they spent lot of time visiting the "Uffizi Gallery" which offered thousands of art works by Michelangelo, Botticelli, Leonardo da Vinci and Titian.

The last visits they paid to "Casa Buonaroti" and the "Leonardo da Vinci" museum.

The children bought many books of art, mentioning that they will read them from time to time, to remember all the splendors they accumulated in that trip.

In the last day of sojourn in Florence, they took the train to Milan and arrived there after three hours. This time the hotel had no walls and ceiling painted; on the ground floor, a stylish lounge bar, and a lovely restaurant, a lounge with a multimedia theme library with glass ceiling that allows the view of a vertical garden, welcomed the guests. Their suite had a spectacular terrace overlooking the rooftops of the old civic center. Same as before, they first took a walk in the neighborhood to become familiar with the surroundings. Milan is a metropolitan city and shopping boutiques and stores are almost on every street. Ana suggested as a must, to buy tickets for the Scala Opera, and everybody agreed with big enthusiasm. They barely could find tickets at the second balcony for Verdi's "Don Carlo" which was scheduled after three days. In the meantime, they took a three-hour walking tour with a guide, to visit landmarks like "Sforza Castle", "Piazza della Scala", the famous "Via Dante", and the spectacular "Milan Cathedral", which is the fifth largest Christian church in the world. It is covered with spires and statues, giving it an unusual look. The construction of the cathedral started in 1386 and was built over several hundred years in a number of contrasting styles and the quality of the workmanship varies markedly, and it is still not finished. They say there are more statues on this gothic-style cathedral than any other building in the world. There are 3,400 statues, 135 gargoyles and 700 figures that decorate Milan Duomo. There are 52 pillars inside Milan Cathedral, one for every week of the year. One of the highlights of the interior of the church is a statue, which depicts Saint Bartholomew. He was skinned alive and is shown standing with his skin draped around him.

The next day was dedicated exclusively to Leonardo da Vinci's "Last Supper" and "The Church of Santa Maria delle Grazie". For the first time, they could appreciate the masterpiece of Leonardo in reality, which is usually distorted in books and reproductions.

Before entering the Opera House, one hour prior to curtain time, they visited the museum, which hosts a vast collection of costumes, instruments, and other musical curiosities, as well as a gallery of busts and paintings portraying some of classical music's greatest artists. The interior of the Opera House can accommodate two thousand spectators and has six tiers of boxes and two galleries above. The artistic splendor of the inside was overwhelming, and in that night the auditorium was crowded to its capacity. The spectacle featured very best voices and went off brilliantly in every respect.

The children were so excited that they kept talking a long time about that night especially that they understood very well the lyrics.

The week for their sojourn in Milan went by, and time for traveling to Venice was there. They took the train and after two hours and a half they arrived at the station and a cab took them to their hotel that was located in the center of the city on the Grand Canal, and was built in the fifteen century. The suite had a view looking across the water to "Santa Maria della Salute", one of Venice's greatest churches, and to the "Palazzo Venier dei Leoni", home to the "Guggenheim Museum". The rooms displayed precious antiques, paintings, frescoes, objects d'art and beautiful fabrics.

They visited first the church across the water, which displayed paintings by Veronese, Tintoretto, and Rubens. It still had an atmosphere of a place of worship, not so much found in other churches that housed art displays. In the same day they visited the collection of modern art housed in the "Guggenheim Museum".

The next day they went to visit the "Doges' Palace" built in Venetian Gothic style, where the frescoes of mythological subjects and of the cities and regions under Venetian dominion painted by Tintoretto from 1578 onwards, were the most impressive.

The children wanted to try a little excursion on the canal by canoe or vaporetto. Ana booked a guide tour to Murano Glass and Burano Lace by vaporetto. Situated just across the Venetian Lagoon from Venice, the islands of Murano and Burano are world-renowned for their traditional artisan crafts. At the Murano Glass making shop, a master gave them a short demonstration, explaining the working process. From the gift shop, Ana bought a pair of beautiful, big glasses for Mili and one pair for Bena. The Burano Island was very picturesque; the buildings were all painted in different colors and charming. They went into the lace shop and looked at the lace master hand making lace, and were very impressed by the skill shown to them. Ana bought a superb set of six handkerchiefs for Mili and one for Brenda. The children took many pictures of everything they saw in that day and talked a lot about that new experience.

When Ana gave Bena the gifts she bought for her, Bena said:

"I don't know how to thank you in simple words."

"I'll tell you in simple words just that: you are to me a mother like Mili is, and you both are grandmothers to my children."

Brenda started crying, embraced Ana and kissed her.

Back at the hotel, they had a hearty dinner at the restaurant and planned the schedule for the next day.

Among other sites, the brochure recommended the Music Museum where they could admire an impressive collection of cellos and violins from the 17th to 19th century. They went there, and after visiting the museum, Ana bought tickets to the evening concert where a local orchestra and soloist played Saint-Saëns *Rondò Capriccioso for violin and strings.* It was a real treat, especially for Lisi, who was captivated by the music and interpretation.

The last day of that memorable vacation was there, and it was time for them to go home. They took the train to Rome and boarded the night flight right on schedule. Before boarding the plane, the three of them embraced Ana and expressed their many thanks for everything she gave them in that unforgettable vacation.

Early in the morning, Mili waited for them at the airport. Bena rushed into her arms and both started crying. The children and Ana embraced her with love telling how much they missed her. After such a long vacation filled with all the splendors and novelties they experienced, being home felt good and somehow easier.

Not only Ana gave her mother the beautiful things she bought for her, but also the children and Bena gave her many souvenirs from those wonderful places they visited. It was Saturday when they returned home, the children had two more weeks vacation but Ana had to go to work on Monday. Over the weekend, they all shared impressions and memories of those splendid moments they spent far from home especially telling Mili stories about everything.

The children were already fifteen years old and they started the tenth grade. Before going to school Ana asked them not to tell stories about their vacation to their classmates, since many of them were poor, could not afford something like that, and they might feel uncomfortable. The children understood very well what their mother said. Lisi asked:

"What should we tell them if they want to know?"

"You can say that most of the time you spent outdoors, and this is not a lie. If they insist, you know how to change the subject."

One day Ana asked Bena:

"I think that some exercise will be good for me, and maybe I should enroll in a program at the gym. What do you think?"

"Excellent idea" Bena said, "it will do you very good, since otherwise you don't exercise at all. When are going to start?"

"I'll go tomorrow and see what schedule they have."

The next day she went to the gym, and asked the trainer to enroll her in the karate program. They agreed on the terms and she will attend the class twice a week making sure that her schedule will not coincide with their children's one. At home, she did not mention anything about karate, and told her family that she was very pleased with the program of exercises that her trainer explained her.

In short time, Ana proved to be a quick learner and a very ambitious student, since she already mastered many moves of the karate skill. Even her trainer was amazed by the progress made by that woman who was in her early forties.

Winter time was already there, and one day the children said that they were invited to a party celebrating the birthday of one of their classmates. Ana asked them:

"Will be a chaperon there?"

"Her parents will be there all the time. Is this enough for a chaperon?"

"I suppose so. You can go, Bena will drive you there, and I'll come and take you home, and this will be no late than nine o'clock."

Adi shaved his moustache and asked his mother:

"You think I should let it grow?"

"Not when you're in high school, my dear. Later on, you can do whatever you like about your moustache."

They bought a present for the birthday girl, and the party was a success, as both Lisi and Adi said. Not very long after, Ana asked them:

"Have you thought about the career you like to pursue? Adi first since you are four minutes older than your sister."

"Yes, I will study Art History and Architecture, and become an Architect, combining all those teachings in my career."

"It is admirable and I couldn't be more proud of you. How about you, Lisi?"

"I will study Languages and become college professor of Literature and Foreign Languages."

"You make me no less proud than your brother. Both of you are outstanding in every thing you perform and this is the biggest reward for me in my life. You don't have the slightest idea what it means for me to see you both thinking and behaving with such maturity at your age."

In the coming summer vacation, there was no more trip overseas, but only short excursions by car, not far from the city. Everybody had many tasks to do at home, and Ana took advantage of her free time to catch up with her reading and spent hours in the kitchen cooking next to Bena. The children followed their programs of music, gym, and reading books that were of great interest for them. One day, Lisi told her mother:

"Adi has a girlfriend and he likes her."

"And Lisi has a boyfriend in the last grade", Adi said.

"Well, why don't you bring them home? I will like very much to meet them," said Ana.

"Why? Because you want to measure their level of intellect? Adi asked.

"Not at all. This is for you to consider, and not for me. I am just trying to be sympathetic and a supportive mother."

The next day, both came with their friends, Linda McMillan and Ryan Kent. Linda came that year from another school and was very well received by her new classmates. Ana liked them and had a long talk about school, plans for the future, hobbies, but very little about families. It was for all of them a very pleasant conversation and that meeting enchanted everybody.

Shortly after, Ana found out from her children that Ryan never knew his father, was abandoned by his mother when he was a toddler, and was raised by his grandmother. Linda's parents were divorced and had shared custody of their daughter. Both Linda and Ryan started to come often to the house, where they liked mostly the big library and music collection. Ana and Bena became fond of them, and appreciated a lot their company. Many times Lisi and Adi played music, which gave everybody a feeling of warmth that was shared with great joy. Besides, their new friends were both very good looking and well educated. Ana asked them one day, about their intentions regarding their career. Linda wanted to study Art and become Interior Designer, while Ryan, wanted to study Art and Design, becoming Book Illustrator, and aspired to develop a career as a writer.

Another year passed by, Lisi, Adi, and Linda entered the twelfth year of school, while Ryan graduated. The entire family attended the graduation ceremony where his grandmother was there also. She was in her late sixties, very pleasant and talkative. At the prom, families were not allowed to attend the party, but the youngsters had a tremendous time to chat about for a long while.

Ryan entered his first year of college, and in the meantime, they all enrolled in a driving school and graduated from there in only one month. Their relationship to each other over time became stronger, trustworthy, and more mature. Somehow, they all became one family, to care about each other, and to share time, feelings, and favorite activities. Ana, Emily, and Brenda could not be happier.

Linda introduced her parents to her new family. Both were very good looking, sophisticated, and seemed to care a lot about their daughter. Ana liked them, hoping to maintain a friendly relationship with them.

In that year, after graduation, Ana bought a small car for Lisi to be shared with Ryan, and one alike for Adi to be shared with Linda. The youngsters exploded of happiness, all four embraced Ana, kissing her and dancing around her. They had more freedom to drive around and not be dependent on someone else for taking them from one place to another. In fall, Lisi, Adi, and Linda enrolled in college and started their first year.

In the meantime, Emily retired from her job, sold her house, and moved with her family. Life was smooth and fulfilling for everybody giving each a sense of plenitude with fresh expectations through the course of a more rewarding existence.

Four more years passed by. The youngsters finished college and all graduated with honor. Adi and Linda started their jobs with an Architectural firm and could not be happier of working together and being close to each other most of the time. Ryan found a very good position with a Publishing House where he started as a Book Illustrator, having also the opportunity to become a writer. Lisi fulfilled her dream to become a College Professor, teaching foreign languages, and French literature. Shortly after, they got married at the same time. It was a wonderful ceremony with great enjoyment to be remembered for their entire lives. For the time being, they all dwelt at home together with Ana, Mili and Bena since the house was big enough to accommodate every one with sufficient comfort.

One day, Ana summoned the entire family for an important meeting. They all were in the living room waiting with impatience for her to start talking.

"I will make a statement which is addressed to Lisi and Adi, and since we all are one family, everybody should listen, without interrupting me. You both are grown-ups now, able to stand strongly on your feet; you have splendid careers, and a family of your own and great responsibilities. You also, are provided with big trust funds, and a lot of money in saving accounts which brings you security and safety."

She took a big breath and made a pause, before continuing:

"Twenty five years ago, shortly after you were born, I killed your father."

Everybody in the audience was horrified. Ana continued with a stern voice:

"He was very sick and his illness had no cure. I had to put an end to his pain and to prevent any sufferings for us all. I committed a crime and now is the time to turn myself in to the authorities. I broke the laws of society and of life, and I have to submit myself to the righteousness of justice. I carried for all those years a horrible burden in my soul and now is the time for me to restore my dignity and my honor on the highest level of fairness and justice, and live with decency the rest of my days. When I will find out about my new location I will let you know."

Every one cried and tried to embrace her but she kept them at distance. Adi managed to say:

"I am going with you."

"No, dear. This is my show and I intend to play it alone. You are now head of family and you have to take care of everybody."

"You will not last there more than one day."

"Wrong. For the past many years, I learned karate and I am a black belt master. I will survive."

Adi asked with a whispered voice:

"What about your job?"

"I resigned two weeks ago. My colleagues do not know much about me and the old ones are no longer there. Nobody there has to know."

Adi approached her, kneeled, kissed her hands and said:

"Now I know why your hair is all white. It is the reflection of your soul that carried the grieve of your sacrifices for all those years."

She caressed and kissed his head without saying anything.

"What kind of human being are you? We never knew how deep inside your soul, you kept your pains and feelings hidden from us" Lisi whispered.

"I am your mother, and this is all about you have to know."

Ana took a long look at each one of them and said:

"Now I would like you all to go to the study because I have to show you something."

They all went to the study and she rushed outside through the back door, running to the corner of the street. She called Adi on his cell phone:

"I could not say goodbye. Give my love to every one."

Ana heard Adi sobbing and she hung up. She called a cab to take her to the police station.

For the last time Ana looked at her home behind, where she left her family, her love, and her life. Her soul was bleeding when she whispered:

"Farewell"

CHAPTER 3

Dusk

ANA ENTERED THE police station, and went to the front desk where an officer asked her about the reason she came for.

"I came to turn myself in for murdering my husband twenty five years ago."

The officer called his superior, who showed Ana to his office, asked her a few questions, gave her some papers, and told her to make a statement. After she finished, the officer said that next morning she will be escorted to the Court House to see the Judge.

"Until then", he said "you will enjoy our hospitality."

He escorted Ana to a cell and locked her up. It was a cold place with a small bed in the corner and a light bulb above.

The next morning a District Attorney showed up and asked her many questions, but Ana said that she wanted to talk directly to the Judge, since she will plea guilty to the murder charges.

One more night she spent in the cell and the next day she was escorted to the Court House and appeared in front of the Judge, a woman in here fifties without any expression in her eyes. The District Attorney was already there. The Judge asked Ana:

"Do you want a lawyer?"

"No, Your Honor. I am here not to defend myself, but to be judged and sentenced for the murder I committed."

"Very well, then. Tell me your story."

Ana looked directly into her eyes all the time she told her the entire story without missing any details, making sure that she exposed everything which was necessary to unveil the truth. After she finished the Judge said:

"You could very well to stay home with your family and no one would ever have known. Why did you choose to confess the crime you committed? Because you feel guilty?"

"No, I do not feel guilty, and I will do it again without remorse. I broke the moral and social laws and lived with this burden in my soul for a very long time; I only wanted to restore my dignity and my honor, and live with honesty the rest of my days."

"Had I had the liberty to let you go, I certainly would do so. But, I have to enforce the law and sentence you for a murder you committed long time ago, and which in my opinion could have been tried in front of a jury under palliating circumstances. Therefore, I sentence you for First-degree murder to thirty years, without parole and the Department of Correction will assign you to the facility. Do you have anything to ask?"

"Yes, Your Honor, I have to ask a big favor."

"Name it."

"I need that my children not ever know the truth. I do not want them to hate their father, not because he did not deserve it, but only because I do not want them to carry in their soul the ugliest, the worst, and the most destructive feeling one can have. This is the reason I chose not to have a trial by jury."

The Judge took a long look at this mother who gave her life for her children and said:

"I respect you for this. They will never know. The people here in my Court Room are sworn to secrecy. I wish I never tried your case."

She made a sign to the officer to approach and said:

"There is no need to handcuff her. She will not try to escape."

The Judge turned around and left without any other word. The officer escorted Ana to the car saying:

"She is the toughest judge in the Court House. Everybody is scared of her."

"She is fair and this is all that counts."

The first step was to the Department of Correction which was the assessment center where she will get classified into what prison she will be going to. The trip to the Department of Correction took less than one hour, in which time there was no sound of any word. From time to time, the officer looked in the rear mirror to that poor woman, thinking that she will not last in prison, more than a few days. Ana looked through the window, having her own thoughts.

A fat guard escorted Ana inside showing her to a desk where she filled in some papers, gave up her belongings which were only her cell phone and the money she brought with her. She was escorted to a room filled with other inmates, and called as a couple at a time into an area with a low wall, where they stripped naked, were searched and told to squat and cough. They were showered and put into orange scrubs (the uniform of intake prisoners). They were then held in holding cells while prisoners had their picture taken for ID's tattoos recorded and scars examined. They were fingerprinted, given medical, dental and eye examination, interviewed by a psychologist, and tested for educational level. After that, they had to submit visitors and phone list to be approved and they got an assigned pin to call. At the end of the classification process, they had to appear before the Institutional Classification Committee where housing, degree of custody, education, and job shall be decided.

After four days, Ana was assigned to a State Prison with medium security that had no tall stone walls, armed guard towers, or razor wire barriers. It was nine o'clock when she arrived there. The prison housed around three hundred prisoners, with about ten male guards for the outside and more than thirty female guards for the inside. Ana was again stripped naked, searched, and after that, she received a newcomers' kit, a dark green uniform of shirt and pants, and was escorted to her cell through a long corridor with a row of cells with barred doors on one side, and a facing wall on the other side.

Upon initial classification she was assigned to medium custody and was eligible for double cell housing. It was a cell for two inmates, equipped with two bunks and two lockers, and had a sink and a toilet which was hidden behind a small screen. Her cellmate was African-American in her late twenties, good looking, very pleasant and friendly.

"Welcome to your new home", she said "I am Vera."

"Thank you, my name is Ana."

Vera showed her how to make the bed and how to set her kit in the locker. She told Ana that she was convicted of murdering her boyfriend five years ago and has twenty more years to go without parole. Ana told her that she was sentenced to thirty years in prison without parole for killing her husband, but not giving any details. She did not ask who was there before her, because she did not want to know something that might could have scared her.

A female guard came to the door and told Ana that the Warden wanted to see her. She found herself in front of a woman in her late forties, with cold eyes and no expression on her face.

"You are assigned to work as a substitute teacher at the level of first grade of elementary classes, to teach about thirty inmates how to read and write until a full time teacher will be hired. You will start tomorrow morning at eight thirty sharp. Now, go back to your cell."

This was a special program of Adult Basic Education courses which focus on teaching basic literacy, and was not part of the regular school curriculum. Classes were held two hours everyday, while regular school program was scheduled for six hours daily.

Ana was escorted back to her cell, and told Vera all about.

"This is not bad at all" Vera said, "it is much better than mopping the showers or working in the laundry room. I worked there, and only recently I was promoted to work in the kitchen."

She told Ana how the daily schedule has to be followed without any mistakes that might be severely punished. Vera also told Ana that many inmates are very bad people and she should be always careful.

"They will try to test you by provoking you to fight" Vera said, "try not to respond to any provocation, and most of it, never report to the guards. Any report will only make the things worse, and it will be followed by revenge. Just be careful and watch your back."

"Thank you Vera, for telling me all these. I will be very careful."

It was already lunch time and the food was served either in cell or in the cafeteria between twelve thirty and one o'clock. Ana was hungry since her last meal was a day before, and even if she didn't like what was on her tray, she ate everything. After lunch it was leisure time for prisoners who were not engaged in work or studies. At two o'clock Ana went in line to make her phone call to the family, who knew nothing about her since she left home. The phone calls were allowed between two and eight o'clock for only five minutes, and Ana managed to be in line before the other inmates came. She thought that the children are not home by that time, so she called Bena on her cell phone who started crying when she heard Ana's voice.

"Bena please stop crying, I am not dead. Write down what I am about to tell you."

She gave Bena all the information about prison location, days, and hours of visiting and also, that she was allowed to only three visitors at the time and they are not allowed to bring her anything for the time being. She asked about everybody and told her that she is doing well.

"I love you all, and don't ever forget this. Give everybody my love and my warmest thoughts. I have to go now."

Until five thirty Ana had a little leisure time and spent it alone since Vera was still at work. Supper was served in the cafeteria and all the inmates stayed in one line, picked a tray waiting to be filled by the server, and then looked for a place to sit at the table. Ana did everything she saw the others doing, and was about to have her seat, when one of the inmates stretched her leg and made her stumble, while every one around started laughing. Ana forgot all about Vera's advice by not responding to provocation. She grasped the arm of that woman, and twisted it so hard, that she started screaming on her kneels down. The guard showed up and asked what happened. Ana answered:

"Nothing. I just stumbled into the bench and spilled the food."

"Clean up your mess and then come with me" the guard said.

Ana cleaned the mess to the last spot and followed the guard. She escorted Ana to the basement and locked her up in a crummy cell, cold, and without any lights. The only piece of furniture there was the toilet. Ana started to pace the room back and forth several times, then sat down in a corner trying to put her thoughts together, without any success. She only could feel cold and scared.

Rules and regulations are everywhere in an organized society, and they have to be obeyed without any opposition for the good purpose of a smooth development of the community. Prisons run on specific rules and regulations which are strictly obeyed but the judicial system does not rely exclusively on them. Fear is the dominant law in a prison and is everywhere, in every corner, in every spot, and in every mind of every inmate. The judicial system is based on fear in prisons which makes it powerful, successful, and without failure. Fear controls the lives of inmates and makes their confinement to be one of the worst chambers of hell, where minds and souls become frozen and where humanity is forced to disappear.

Ana managed to doze for few minutes, until morning was there and the guard showed at the door:

"Get up, and go to your cell" she said.

She escorted Ana to her cell where Vera already made the beds for both.

"Didn't I tell you not to respond to provocation?"

"Yes, you did but I completely forgot. I'll be more careful."

It was morning roll-call in front of the doors, where all the inmates were aligned like soldiers. After that, they all went in one single line to the cafeteria for breakfast.

A guard came and escorted Ana to a nearby small building where the school was located. She had to be there by eight thirty sharp, and she had to teach the inmates basic literacy, namely reading, writing, and math. About twenty-eight students were already in the class; they were between twenty and thirty years old.

"Good morning", Ana said.

"Good morning", some of them answered.

On her desk was a sheet of paper with the name of the students.

"You will call me 'Teacher', and I shall call you by the name you want to be called. Now, who can read or write, or both, raise your hands."

No one raised hands. Ana took a look at them, and spotted in the last raw the inmate who tried to attack her last night in the cafeteria.

"We will start learning first all twenty-six letters of the alphabet. I will write on the blackboard each letter and you will repeat after me. Letters are written in majuscule or minuscule case and we will learn both at the same time. You will know the correct sound or sounds that each letter makes. Take your notebook and your pencil and write down what you see on the blackboard."

She started with the letter "a, A", asking them to write down and repeat the sound. In those two hours of school, they could repeat the sounds of all the letters.

"Your home work will be for tomorrow to write all the letters as many times until you will feel comfortable with each. Tomorrow in class we will have a test and from there we will see how to go forward."

The bell sounded the end of class. Ana waited for them to leave, when one of them stopped in front of the desk and said:

"I am sorry for making you stumbling last night in the cafeteria."

"What stumbling? I don't know what you're talking about."

They all left and another guard was there to escort Ana to her cell. The next day, she checked their homework and said that she was pleased with the assignment she gave them.

"Now, we'll learn to put letters together and make short words. Who wants to start?"

The one who assaulted her, raised hand first and Ana called her to step forward.

"How do I call you?"

"Denise."

"All right, Denise, write on the blackboard the word 'dog' with majuscule and minuscule letters."

She did well, and other students followed one by one writing what Ana told them. For their next homework she assigned them to write about twenty words for as many times they thought will be comfortable for them.

In that evening Vera asked her how was her day in school and if she had any problems. Ana told her about everything and so far, there were no problems. The inmates showed interest and willingness to learn and that is all that counts.

"Vera, may I ask you a question, and you answer only if you feel comfortable. What is your scholastic level of education?"

"I don't mind at all asking me this question. I dropped off school at the end of seventh grade when I was fourteen years old. Shortly after, I became a prostitute and made my living."

"Would you like to start learning and finish high school? I can help you."

"What for? I am now thirty-two years old and when, and if I'll get out of this place I'll be fifty-two. What will I do with my high school diploma by then?"

"I don't know what you will do by that time. What I know is that you should live with hope and expectations every minute of your present time. You owe to yourself a reward for the time you suffered and missed the opportunities to accomplish any goal for your future."

"Maybe you're right. Maybe I should try. Would you help me?"

"Very willing. First you must fill an application to be tested for the right level of school. You have to see the Warden and tell her your intention to enroll in the program. If you have her approval then I'll help you with everything you will need to learn."

In that day Vera asked the guard to see the Warden, she was escorted to the office, told her the story and received an application. Ana helped her with all the questions she had to answer and next day Vera submitted her request. The time for test was scheduled in two weeks from then and she was classified to attend the seventh grade, even if she already had to be in eighth grade by the time she dropped off school. The library was a good start for reading the books, Ana suggested. Vera started using her free time for learning, and she will attend the class when the school year will begin.

Before that, Saturday around five o'clock, the guard showed at the door, telling Ana that she had visitors and she escorted her to a big room with round tables and chairs. Mili, Lisi, and Adi were there waiting for her. The guard said:

"Hugging, kissing and embracing are allowed for fifteen seconds, at the beginning and end of visits. No bodily contact, except for handholding. You have one hour."

They jumped into each others arms embracing Ana with love, kissing her and crying in the same time. Then they took a seat around the table and everybody wanted to talk first.

"How are you?" they all asked together.

"I miss you more than you can imagine. I miss everything from home. I am alright, according to the situation. I will tell you about me in short words."

She told them about almost everything that was for them to know, especially mentioning her cellmate Vera who was good and kind to her. She told them about the strict schedule and about her job as a substitute teacher at the first grade.

"Now, tell me about you, everything and don't miss any details."

"Not so fast", Adi said "tell us how they treat you here, if you have enough food, and if you need anything that we are allowed to bring. Have you been assaulted or attacked? Did anyone tried to hurt you?"

"No, dear. No one has hurt me and I have not been assaulted. I am treated alright but don't expect any warm feelings from these people who are trained to enforce rules and regulations at any moment. The inmates are grouped according to their level of understanding each others and everybody behaves by following what is supposed to be carried out without objections. Answering to your question, I have enough food and you are not allowed to bring me anything from outside. If you want to treat me now, give me a soda from the vending machine."

Adi brought soda for everybody and told her about his new project that he likes a lot, about his colleagues and about how much he enjoys working for his firm. Linda works with him at the same project and they make good partners in job as they are best partners in marriage.

Ana showed a lot of interest for her son's successes and asked her daughter to tell her story. Lisi was extremely pleased with her position as professor, teaching French Language and Literature at the college. She published already a paper about French literature from the first half of the nineteenth century which was dominated by Romanticism. Ryan proved to be her great love and they help each other sharing everything they have and enjoy.

Ana could not be happier for both her children. It was her mother's turn to tell her story.

"It is not much for me to tell, except that every evening Bena and I, both are waiting for the children to come home and share with us over the dinner we cooked, stories about their work and colleagues. What I really want to tell you, is that we all miss you terribly, and I'm still not accustomed to face such a harsh situation. Next to this, I must say that beside that I love you, I have a great esteem for you, and I greatly admire you for what you did, no matter how much I suffer. Not many people that I know, would have had your courage and dignity to act like you did. My dearest Ana, I know you better than anyone in the whole world, and much better than you can imagine."

"She knows", Ana thought, "but she will never tell them."

Ana touched her hands over the table and pressed them gently. They understood each other's thoughts without any words.

"Thank you Mom, for everything you said and did for me. I appreciate a lot that you understand me so well."

The guard approached and said the visit was over.

"Give my love to Bena, Linda, and Ryan. You all take care of each other," Ana said.

"We love you, Mama" the children said, "take good care of yourself, and we'll see you next Saturday."

They all had a short hug and kissed each other. Ana left first and was escorted to her cell. At the desk outside, the police woman asked them if they want to put money in Ana's account to be available through J-Pay kiosks. All three did.

Back to her cell Ana answered to Vera's questions about her family:

"They all are doing well, every one keeping busy with work and home activities. They miss me and I miss them, but we have to cope with the situation just the way it is."

"My only family left, is my brother who is somewhere in a prison for drug trafficking, and I haven't heard of him in the past five years. I wished having a family, at least knowing where my brother is."

"I cannot substitute for your family," Ana said "but I can be your friend, and you can trust me."

"You mean that? It is very important to me what you said."

"I mean well. I need your friendship too."

"Thank you Ana for being so kind to me and understanding me so well."

The evening roll-call was announced, the doors opened, and every one stepped one foot outside, standing there for a few minutes. Back inside the cell, the lights went off and they went to bed. Before falling asleep, Ana thought about her family, and how much they love each other. Her mother knew from the beginning that she committed a murder and sacrificed her life only to save the lives of her children, but never said a word during those past twenty-five years. Her mother carried a big burden in her soul no less painful than she had to bear. Ana felt a big relief in her mind thinking that she was no longer alone agonizing over her suffering. She fell asleep with a smile on her face.

The wake-up was at six thirty and the day started with the regular schedule, with morning exercises, personal hygiene, and making the beds.

After breakfast they all returned to their cells for the morning roll-call, and then the inmates were escorted to work and school.

In that day, Ana wrote on the blackboard about one hundred longer words, and asked her students to read and spell them. They did quite good, and she was pleased with the progress they made. As homework she told them to read, write, and spell those words until they will feel comfortable.

"Tomorrow, we will have one hour reading and writing, and the next hour we will start math. Who knows about numbers?"

Almost every one raised hands. It was quite natural, since those inmates came from the street where money was the front runner in their lives.

"You make me proud," she said.

They answered with a round of applauses, forgetting for a moment their hardship in that prison.

After lunch, until five o'clock, was leisure time when prisoners were not escorted by guards, they were allowed to spend their free time outside or in a common room playing cards or watching television. Ana needed to call her mother.

"I want to tell you that I thought last night a lot about what you told me when you came here. I want to thank you from the bottom of my soul for understanding me and for your love."

"There is no need to tell me", her mother said "words are not enough to express my feelings and my understanding. This coming Saturday, Bena wants to come with the children and visit you. We'll see each other next time.

"I love you mom. I have to go now."

Ana hung up with a feeling of deep peace in her soul. She went to the library where a woman in her fifties by the name Gilda Mercer, was in charge. She was a professional librarian, very friendly and considerate, and she was from outside. Later on, Ana found out that she was a spinster and her only family was a dog and a cat. The library was open from eleven o'clock in the morning to five o'clock in the afternoon, six days a week; it was quite a big room, with four long tables and chairs on the sides, housing all the furniture to accommodate about thirty to forty people at the same time. The book collection included materials to meet the informational, educational, cultural, recreational, and rehabilitative needs of the prison population. The books were displayed on six rows of bookcases along the room and on shelves along two walls. Six computers were arranged on a long table next to the wall on the right side of the door and they were accessible for informational, educational, and recreational pursuits, but no email was allowed. There was not a single reader by that time. A guard was inside, being replaced every hour.

"May I use the computer?" Ana asked.

"Certainly. How much do you know about computers?"

"I have some knowledge. I promise not to break anything."

"Go ahead and play a little if you like it."

Ana looked for the site of her place of work, the Institute of Immunology. She published many papers along the years that were praised in the scientific community. She found the site, and there was her name mentioned as a valuable researcher with great contribution to the Immunology field. All her papers were there, and dear memories came to her mind. Ana had tears in her eyes and for a moment she completely forgot where she was. Gilda was behind her, looking at the site, and asked:

"Did you find what you looked for? It seems to me that you are very familiar with the article."

"Yes, I am and thank you very much."

Ana turned off the site and left. It was like yesterday when she was in the lab doing research, and yet her feelings were like suspended in a time without measure, that could not be counted anymore. She went to supper and then took a shower, and went to her cell. After evening roll-call she went to bed. Memories of her childhood came one by one in her mind. She thought about her grandparents, way back in time, when she was a little girl and they told her many stories. Ana was named by her maternal grandmother; Andrew was named by her maternal grandfather and Elise by her paternal grandmother. She remembered them when they came to the house and always brought her toys and sweets, joked with her and made her laugh. They died one by one when she was about the kindergarten age, and it was hard for her to understand what death was, even if her parents tried to give her an explanation for her age. She only knew that they will never come back from where they were gone, and she had a feeling of a big loss.

Before falling asleep that night, Ana thought about her very early childhood which was a wonderful time in her life. A terrifying scream woke her up abruptly, and Vera told her that many times inmates have terrible nightmares and they scream or cry, and nobody will help them to calm down. Ana thought that one more aspect of fear shows up and hurts a life in that territory of hell.

The next day was like the one before, and hopefully like the coming ones, if nothing threatening will appear. Saturday was already there, when time for her visitors was announced by the guard. Her children and Bena embraced and kissed her with warmth and love.

"You all look wonderful", Ana said "how is everybody in the family?"

"Mili, Linda, and Ryan miss you and send you their love", Lisi said "we all are doing alright, but nothing home is the same since you left. We talk a lot about you and how was our life when you were home."

"Let's say just that it was different" Ana said, "how are you my second dear mother, Bena?"

"I miss you a lot, and feel your presence in the house all the time, waiting for you to come home from work, expecting you to come out of the study, coming to the kitchen to taste the food, and so on. What else can I say?"

"Bena is right, Mama" Adi said, "we feel your presence all the time in the house."

Ana wanted to change the subject or otherwise everybody would start crying.

"I think you and Lisi should make a trip to Heidelberg and sell the house. It is about time and you will make a lot of money."

"No need for that" Adi said "I already talked to the lawyer who takes care of the inheritance; he will find a buyer and sell the house without us being there. I'll let you know. Now, tell us about you."

"I went yesterday to the library, they have six computers there, and I visited the site of the Institute, where my name was listed as a prominent researcher with many published papers. You can imagine how touched I was."

"I saw the site too" Adi said "and I was immensely proud of you. They gave you a tremendous recognition."

Time for visit was over and everybody had to leave. They embraced each other, promising to come next Saturday in a different formation.

"You don't have to come every Saturday. Once or maybe twice a month will be enough for me and for you. Think about and find something better to do."

"We love you, and take care of yourself. What we do with our time is not anymore of your concern" Lisi said.

Ana left first, escorted by the guard. She went outside in the courtyard for a fresh breath and a walk. Some of the inmates were in groups, talking, playing ball, or exercising, some others walked along the high walls, alone or grouped. In a corner she saw Vera sitting on the floor reading a book.

"Hello, friend. Come with me for a walk. It will do you good."

"Hello, friend, I was all day long on my feet and had enough exercise. I have to study this chapter of Botany on pollination of plants. I have to review all the material for my test. You go and have a good walk, and I'll see you tonight."

Ana went for a walk along the wall, when a couple joined her. One of them said:

"The girls in your class said that you are a good teacher and they like you."

"I'm very pleased to hear that. Just doing my job the best I can. They all are good people willing to learn."

They walked together for a while, talking about casual subjects, like their places of work, leisure time, and nothing of a particular meaning. The evening roll-call was close and they had to return to their cells.

That night before going to sleep, old memories of her childhood came to Ana's mind. She remembered well when she was in preschool, and one day a boy tried to kiss her. She became so angry that she punched him in his face and the boy's nose started bleeding. They both were suspended for two days. Her father, who usually was on her side, approved what she did without any other comment. On the other hand, her mother said that she could have used a milder attitude and not hurt the poor boy. Somehow, Ana understood that both her parents could be right, even if she didn't know how being gentle and angry could work together in the same time. In any case, that boy or any other never tried to kiss her again. In one of those days of her suspension, her mother took her to the hospital where she worked, and Ana met a few very sick children about her age. They were pleased to talk to her, showed her their toys, and asked her to come again. In that day Ana was sad, thinking that those children will never be healthy again. She asked her mother if they are going to die, because they looked so pale and without any strength when they were talking. Her mother said that with proper and continuous treatment many of them will be out of the hospital in good time. The main reason she took Ana to visit them was to show her a site of life that was totally different from what Ana knew. She also told her that the most important feelings in her soul should be compassion, kindness, and love for every single human being who is suffering and needs help. It was the first lesson for Ana from the many others of the same kind that her mother gave her in that day. She fell asleep with a feeling of peace in her soul.

Next day in class, her students showed progress in their homework of reading and writing and it was time to start math. They all knew about numbers to add and subtract them but nothing about fractions and multiplications. They understood very quickly what Ana showed them on the blackboard starting with simple computations. Math exercises were added to their assignment of reading and writing for the next day homework.

As every day, Ana was escorted back to her cell. She had nothing to do except for preparing the school material for the next day. She needed some stationery like notebooks and pens, and for that she had to fill in a request form and ask approval from the Warden. The guard was walking outside the door; Ana called her and told her what she needed.

"Let's go see the Warden" she said.

The guard entered the room and told something to the woman with cold eyes and no expression on her face who was working on some papers. Ana stood at the door waiting for her to speak first.

"What do you need?"

"I need to buy ten notebooks and thirty pens."

"Why?"

"I think to sketch my biography."

"Fill in this request form and sign it."

Ana did what the Warden said, and the guard escorted her back to her cell. She thought that it wasn't that hard to get the approval for her request. After lunch it was leisure time and she went to the library. Gilda was at her desk and a couple of inmates were looking at the books on the first row of bookcases. Ana took a place in front of a computer and started searching for a web site. One of the inmates approached her and asked to write an email for her.

"There is no email allowed" Ana said.

The girl slapped her on the back of the head such that Ana's glasses sprang on the table.

"Now it's allowed" she said.

Ana stood up and in three moves put her down. The guard rushed and asked:

"Is she dead?"

"No, she will be alright in a couple of minutes. She asked a question and I gave her the wrong answer. Just a minor mix–up. Nothing to worry about."

The girl stood up and the guard told her to get out and never come to the library on her watch. Ana continued her search for latest information on a project she worked at the institute, and found that some progress was made since she left.

It was time to call her family and she chose Lisi that day.

"Randy and Mili will come with me to see you this Saturday. I found a shortcut that takes only about thirty-five minutes to get there."

"I'll be happy as usually to see you, but you know, you don't have to come. I can call you everyday."

"Don't mention it. I have some news for you."

"Give my love to all, and take care one of another. I have to go now."

Ana went to supper and then outside for a walk. Vera joined her this time and told her that next week she had to take the test for being admitted to school. She felt confident thanks to Ana's help and hoped that she will pass it.

Next day early in the morning before going to work, the guard told Ana that the Warden wanted to see her. She was escorted there and waited at the door to find out why she was called for. The unpleasant woman told her to approach the desk and said:

"A fulltime teacher from outside will replace you since the class will have the same schedule as the regular school, starting tomorrow. The librarian needs help and she asked for you. You are assigned to the library and you will start tomorrow your new job. You can go now."

Ana was about to explode of joy, but she didn't say a word. She was escorted directly to the school for the last time. After class, she told her students about her replacement and said:

"I enjoyed a lot working with you and I want you to promise me that you will keep learning, doing your homework, and making progress in everything you will be taught. You will learn many new courses that you will like. You all are good people and you deserve to go further to achieve your goal in having a better future."

They all stood up and gave her a round of applauses.

In that day Ana felt like singing and jumping all the time. She went to her cell, thinking that somehow she was assigned to the best place of work in that establishment. After lunch she went to the library.

"I saw your background and asked the Warden for you to help me in the library" Gilda said.

"I thank you very much for trusting me and I promise not to disappoint you. The Warden said that I should start tomorrow but I can start now."

"You will be in charge mostly with the computers, but first we'll have to update the inventory, which is overdue. We cannot close the library for this purpose, so that we have to deal with the situation just the way it is. We'll start tomorrow at eleven o'clock."

In that evening Ana told Vera about her new assignment which was the best thing that happened to her since she came. Vera was indeed very happy for her and also told Ana that she heard how she overpowered the inmate who assaulted her.

"You acquired quite a reputation around. Too bad that you are not allowed to teach me Karate. I would love to learn it."

"It took me many years to master it, but it seems that the time I spent learning was worthy after all."

The next morning Ana was escorted to her new place of work. All the information regarding the library was stored in a computer placed on a small desk next to the window. Gilda gave her the password and showed her how to proceed with the inventory. There were many books piled up in a corner that had to be included in the data sheet, for which a program had to be used. It was a very easy task for Ana to perform since she had a big experience with computers, mostly with registering data from her studies. The books came from donations and most of them were of educational and cultural topics. In that day Ana managed to register about half of them and arrange them on the shelves in the required order. Gilda was very pleased with the results and told her that she can use the email every time she needed.

"Thank you, but I don't have to use email since I talk almost every day with my family and I see my children every Saturday."

Gilda showed her the data sheet regarding the names of all inmates, and told her the procedure of borrowing books, mentioning the instructions to be followed in registering the day for taking the books out and the day of returning them. She also told Ana the rules to be followed by inmates regarding the use of computers.

It was closing time for that day. Ana went to supper and then outside for a walk. In that evening the guard brought her the stationery she asked for. She put everything in her locker and thought that maybe one of those days she will start writing probably not more than one page at the time.

The next day she finished to register all the remaining books and arrange them in the right places. There were still many empty spots and she thought that some art books will be maybe well received. The library was updated, well organized, waiting for visitors to take advantage of the book collection, according to their needs and tastes.

It was Saturday and time for visit. Mili, Lisi, and Ryan were already there waiting for her. After embracing each other, Ana told Ryan to talk first since she didn't see him in a long time. He published his first book with children stories that he also illustrated.

"Lisi knows hundreds o stories learned from you and I intend to use most of them for writing children books, that I also will illustrate. This is what I like most to do with my profession."

"Congratulations Ryan, I am very proud of you. The stories I told Lisi and Adi were part real and part imagined; most important was that they liked them a lot and never had enough of them. You will make an impressive career because you love what you are doing. Now Lisi tell me about the news you mentioned on the phone."

"The house in Heidelberg was sold for a high price and now we are richer. I asked Adi permission to tell you the best news of all and he said that since we are twins it doesn't matter who tells you first: Linda is pregnant."

Ana was stirred by excitement, asking every question she could think about. They didn't know if it is a girl or a boy, since it was too early for a sonogram.

"The house next door on our left side is for sale and Adi wants to buy it, since now the family is growing and we need more space" Lisi said.

"This is a very good idea. How about Mili and Bena?"

"I shall stay with these two, and Bena will move with Adi and Linda when the baby comes", her mother answered.

"We will be close to each others all the time like living in the same house", Ryan said "actually, we cannot be ones without the others. Every evening over dinner each of us tells the story of the day, sharing knowledge, impressions, and feelings with the rest of the family."

"You all make me happy", Ana said "and most of all you make my life easier to bear in this place."

She told them about her work in the library that was the best thing which could happen to her. They all knew, even if not much, how hard the life in that prison was, but for a change Ana had a better place to work than all the other inmates. She asked them to give her love to Adi and Linda, embraced the three of them, and left.

Ana went outside for a walk until evening roll-call. Before falling asleep she had a sense of fulfilling a lifelong dream of her family being strong, resolute, and not depending or contingent upon something else for existence.

The next day, an inmate approached Ana in the library, saying that she needs her help in preparing the hearing for the parole board.

"Let's do this together. What is your name?"

"Sandra, and I'm eligible to appear in front of the board, but I need help to understand how to defend my case."

Ana searched the web site with all the information regarding the parole board, and explained her every single paragraph of what she was supposed to do. Nothing was simple there, but Sandra understood enough to prepare her case. Ana gave her a print with the information and told her to read it several times and memorize every indication included. It turned out that at the hearing Sandra did very well and her parole was approved. Ana was glad that she could help someone to get out of that place. After a few days, Vera showed up in the library.

"I couldn't wait until tonight to tell you that I passed the test and I'm enrolled in school which will start next month."

"Congratulations with all my warmest feelings. It is a little early to ask you but I would like to know what your plans are after finishing high school?"

"I don't see why I should go farther. A diploma of high school will be enough for me, just as you said that it will be my reward for the life I had."

"Do you want to go back to the kitchen after high school?"

"No, I wouldn't like that, but maybe they will find a place of work for me somewhere else."

"What do you feel like becoming a teacher for the elementary grades? You need to enroll in college through mail correspondence and after you get the degree you can become a 'Teacher Aide' assisting the instructor in the classroom."

"I like very much your idea, and now I have to think of such a perspective for me, if you will help me realize it in the coming future."

"I am always here for you and I will help you all the way. Let's take a look just out of curiosity what the computer says."

Ana searched the site with all information regarding credentials and courses for teacher degree through mail correspondence. It was a pleasure for both of them to search and learn about rules and conditions regarding what Vera needed for achieving a teaching career.

"In the meantime", Ana said "I shall teach you everything you need to know about using the computer for doing homework, learning what you will find interesting and searching online for all the information you wish to access.

"You changed my life, and I don't know how to thank you enough. You pulled me out of a hole where

I lived like a vegetable all my life. How am I ever be able to thank you?"

"Just being my friend. Monday we'll start the computer first lesson."

That evening both continued talking until they fell asleep.

In the coming Saturday, Mili, Lisi, and Adi came to visit. They all competed in telling Ana the best news, that Linda expected a girl and Lisi was pregnant.

"I am breathless", Ana said "and I don't have enough words to express my feelings. I wished the circumstances would be different, but we cannot change anything in this regard. Even so, my heart is always with you all, and I want you to know that there is no one in the whole world that is able to love you more than me. My thoughts and my warmest feelings are always with you."

In that night she had a lot more to think about her family. Ana knew that she will never see her grandchildren since she will never allow them to come in that horrible place. Whatever their parents will decide to tell them about their grandmother, will be much better for them than knowing the truth. A deep feeling of sadness covered her troubled soul. She remembered clearly the voice which once said to her: "Joy and suffering both go together, side by side, and touch the same chord. All depends on the stimulus that is triggered by the mind and is activated first."

In the coming week a new group of inmates checked in. They all were murderers, and they were wild. Over a few days only, many of them committed already assaults and were sent to the basement to enjoy the hospitality of hell. Probably in time, they will understand the hard way that there was no place for them to go, and they will learn how to obey the rules if they wanted to survive.

Vera started her first computer lesson, and Ana was surprised how easy she understood from the beginning what that marvelous machine can do.

"I like it so much", Vera said "that I will come every single day to learn after my work shift. Until now, only the word 'computer' scared me terribly."

"It will be a good friend if you know its language. It will give you every bit of knowledge that you need at any time you will ask. I prepared a sheet with terms and explanation of each word for you to become familiar with the system and communication. Read it and memorize as much as you can and then we'll practice together."

Vera came to the library every day as she said and in short time she was able to master the computer basics. Not long after, she could surf the internet for the sites connected to the school. At night in the cell she shared her enthusiasm with Ana who was very pleased with the progress of her learning and the knowledge she accumulated.

After two weeks the school started, Vera was no longer working in the kitchen; she was enrolled in seventh grade full time and was always enthusiastic about the new aspect of her life.

Christmas was already there, but no holiday celebration was allowed. Just a little better food at diner in the cafeteria was all that the inmates received. It was snowing outside displaying a beautiful, peaceful scenic view for every one to enjoy, and perhaps that was a minute of time when mental strain was set aside for awhile.

Time went by again, one day was no different from another, a season to harden was no different from another, and a year was the same as the one before. Time was just one leaf after another of a calendar pad with no different patterns of feelings or memories to be treasured and remembered.

In the next year, Adi and Linda had a baby girl and named her Ana. Bena moved with them taking with her all the memories she had in the old house. After one month Lisi and Ryan had a baby boy and named him Matthew. Mili stayed with them taking charge of the entire household.

In the meantime, Ana kept writing her book mentioning all the details she could remember, with comments and picturesque description about her family and the people who were part of her life.

Over the passing years, her family came less and less to see her. Emily died and Adi asked the Warden to let Ana attend the funerals for her mother. She was escorted by the guard to the cemetery and nobody noticed the prison car that was parked farther away. There in that casket she looked for the last time at the image of her beloved mother who was her educator, her confidant, and her best friend. Ana joined hands with her twin children and together expressed their love to the most kind, generous, and honest human being they ever knew.

Back to the prison, Ana carried one more suffering in her soul, trying to deal with her harsh reality, not even knowing what for. Her children had their own families to take care, they had a good and prosperous life, and they had no longer need for her.

She built for them a solid and enduring path of life, with love and compassion, with fairness and justice. Her image will be in their souls and on every step of the road for their entire life. She kept her promise and she fulfilled her oath that was blessed with His Grace by the Creator.

Ana was alone in a place where feelings and memories of the past had to be streamed out carefully, such as not to be touched by the hostile environment in which she was constraint to live.

After two more years, Brenda died, taking with her the love and warmth of the people who were her family and her friends. It was no one left of the people who already fulfilled their duties and commitments without failure, and who left behind their honesty and sense of justice to be carried further by the young generation who inherited their treasures of moral values.

We live in a limited world with boundaries that cannot be trespassed. Our reality is made of small and distinctive pieces with borders that cannot be cut across, like a jigsaw puzzle where every shape with a particular design fits together into the whole picture. Our realities make our world, the only one that we can understand and therefore we can accept. It is the only world that is proven by science to be true in our life, and therefore we can trust. When thinking about an eternal existence, faith comes in and takes over our judgment. If there is such a world, then it must be unlimited, without boundaries and where time has no measure. Logically we cannot understand it and therefore we cannot accept it. In the same time it is hard to think that our limited world that we know has to end one day or the other and our life shaped by our real thoughts and feelings will disappear without leaving any trace. We do not know if eternity exists, but we still can make a compromise between science and faith and accept doubt as part of the mechanism that can put closer if not together two worlds that seem to be so far from each other.

In that night of no particular date, Ana tried to clear her thoughts and put together memories of her past in a way that everything coming to her mind to be distinct and beyond a shadow of doubt. Places, events, people, family, paraded before her eyes, stirring with accuracy the feelings she had in every moment of those times. The complexity of her life narrowed down to only a few features that still could be active. Her real world was reduced to only a few pieces of the jigsaw puzzle with a whole picture of a very small design showing a single snowflake without any borders, since all the boundaries were broken toward a space and time that had no longer dimensions and measurements.

From somewhere, from a long time gone by, came to her the sound of a violin playing the music of her life. Her mind was clear of doubt, and her soul full of love and compassion found serenity and peace when she whispered:

"Farewell"

Printed in the United States
By Bookmasters